William T. Sherman

General Sherman's Official Account of his Great March Through

Georgia and the Carolinas

from his departure from Chattanooga to the surrender of General Joseph E.

Johnston and the Confederate forces under his command

William T. Sherman

General Sherman's Official Account of his Great March Through Georgia and the Carolinas
*from his departure from Chattanooga to the surrender of General Joseph E. Johnston and the
Confederate forces under his command*

ISBN/EAN: 9783337780661

Printed in Europe, USA, Canada, Australia, Japan

Cover: Foto ©Andreas Hilbeck / pixelio.de

More available books at **www.hansebooks.com**

GENERAL SHERMAN'S

OFFICIAL ACCOUNT

OF HIS

GREAT MARCH

THROUGH GEORGIA AND THE CAROLINAS,

FROM HIS DEPARTURE FROM CHATTANOOGA TO THE SUR-
RENDER OF GENERAL JOSEPH E. JOHNSTON AND
THE CONFEDERATE FORCES UNDER
HIS COMMAND.

TO WHICH IS ADDED,

GENERAL SHERMAN'S EVIDENCE BEFORE THE CONGRESSIONAL
COMMITTEE ON THE CONDUCT OF THE WAR;
THE ANIMADVERSIONS OF SECRETARY
STANTON AND GENERAL HALLECK:

WITH

A DEFENCE OF HIS PROCEEDINGS, ETC.

NEW YORK:
BUNCE & HUNTINGTON, PUBLISHERS.
1865.

PREFACE.

————◆•◆————

THE national interest attached to General Sherman's great campaign in the Southern States,—one of the most brilliant and remarkable military achievements in history,—induces the publishers to present, in readable type and compact form, its story as it is told in the words of the gallant hero. The narrative, to adopt the comment upon it of a military critic, is written in "a terse, vigorous, and picturesque style." It will well repay perusal, and cannot fail to convince the reader that power and accuracy of description are not among the least accomplishments of this distinguished soldier.

To render the record complete, General Sherman's Official Report is followed by his correspondence with General Joseph E. Johnston, his testimony before the Congressional Committee on the Conduct of the War, and official and other animadversions passed upon him, in consequence of his original agreement with General Johnston. The latter will be found

fully answered in a defence of his proceedings subjoined, attributed to the pen of his brother, Senator
Sherman, as well as in the Report and evidence of
the General himself

CONTENTS.

GENERAL SHERMAN'S

OFFICIAL ACCOUNT

OF HIS

GREAT MARCH

THROUGH GEORGIA AND THE CAROLINAS.

———————·

I.

FROM CHATTANOOGA TO ATLANTA.

Headquarters Military Division of the Mississippi,
Atlanta, Ga., September 15, 1864.

General—I have heretofore, from day to day, by telegraph, kept the War Department and the General-in-Chief advised of the progress of events; but now it becomes necessary to review the whole campaign which has resulted in the capture and occupation of the city of Atlanta.

On the 14th day of March, 1864, at Memphis, Tennessee, I received notice from General Grant at Nashville that he had been commissioned Lieutenant-General and Commander-in-Chief of the Armies of the United States, which would compel him to go East, and that I had been appointed to succeed him as commander of the Division of the Mississippi. He summoned me to Nashville for a conference, and I took my departure the same day, and reached Nashville, *via* Cairo, on the 17th, and accompanied him on his journey eastward as far as Cincinnati. We had a full and complete understanding of the policy and plans for the ensuing campaign, covering a vast area of country, my part of which extended from Chattanooga to Vicksburg. I returned to Nashville, and on the 25th began a tour of inspection, visiting Athens, Decatur, Huntsville, and Larkin's Ferry, Alabama; Chattanooga, Loudon, and Knoxville, Tennessee. During this visit I had interviews with Major-General McPherson, commanding the Army of the Tennessee, at Huntsville; Major-General Thomas, commanding the Army of the Cumberland, at Chattanooga; and Major-General Schofield, commanding the Army of the Ohio, at Knoxville. We arranged in general terms the lines of communication to be guarded, the strength of the several columns and garrisons, and fixed the 1st day of May as the time when all things should be ready. Leaving these officers to complete the details of organization and preparation, I returned to Nashville on the 2d of April, and gave my personal attention to the question of supplies. I found the depots at Nashville abundantly supplied, and the railroads in very fair order, and that steps had already been taken to supply cars and locomotives to fill the new and increased demands of the service; but the impoverished condition of the inhabitants of East Tennessee, more especially in the region round about Chattanooga, had forced the commanding officers of posts to issue food to the people. I was compelled to stop this, for a simple calculation showed that a single railroad could not feed the armies and the people too, and of course the army had the preference; but I endeavored to point the people to new channels of supply. At first my orders operated very hardly, but the prolific soil soon afforded early vegetation, and ox-wagons hauled meat and bread from Kentucky, so that no actual suffering resulted; and I trust that those who clamored at the cruelty and hardships of the day have already seen in the result a perfect justification of my course. At once the storehouses at Chattanooga began to fill, so that by the 1st of May a very respectable quantity of food and forage had been accumulated there; and from that day to this stores have been brought forward in wonderful abundance, with a surplus that has enabled me to feed the army well during the whole period of time, although the enemy has succeeded more than once in breaking our road for many miles at different points.

During the month of April I received from Lieutenant-General Grant a map, with a letter of instructions, which is now at Nashville; but a copy will be procured, and made part of this report. Subsequently I received from him notice that he would move from his camps about Culpepper, Virginia, on the 5th of May, and he wanted me to do the same from Chattanooga. My troops were still dispersed, and the cavalry, so necessary to our success, was yet collecting horses at Nicholasville, Kentucky, and Columbus, Tennessee. On the 27th of April I put all the troops in motion towards Chattanooga, and on the next day went there in person. My aim and purpose was to make the Army of the Cumberland 50,000 men, that of the Tennessee 35,000, and that of the Ohio 15,000. These figures were approximated but never reached, the Army of the Tennessee failing to receive certain divisions that were still kept on the Mississippi, resulting from the unfavorable issue of the Red River expedition. But on the 1st of May the effective strength of the several armies for offensive purposes was about as follows :

ARMY OF THE CUMBERLAND—MAJOR-GENERAL THOMAS COMMANDING.

Infantry	54,568
Artillery	2,377
Cavalry	3,828
Total	60,773
Guns	130

ARMY OF THE TENNESSEE—MAJOR-GENERAL McPHERSON COMMANDING.

Infantry	22,437
Artillery	1,404
Cavalry	624
Total	24,465
Guns	96

ARMY OF THE OHIO—MAJOR-GENERAL SCHOFIELD COMMANDING.

Infantry	11,183
Artillery	679
Cavalry	1,697
Total	13,559
Guns	28
Grand aggregate number of troops	98,797
Guns	254

About these figures have been maintained during the campaign, the number of men joining from furlough and hospitals about compensating for the loss in battle and from sickness. These armies were grouped on the morning of May 6th as follows: That of the Cumberland at and near Ringgold; that of the Tennessee at Gordon's Mill, on the Chickamauga; and that of the Ohio near Red Clay, on the Georgia line, north of Dalton.

The enemy lay in and about Dalton, superior to me in cavalry (Wheeler's), and with three corps of infantry and artillery, viz., Hardee's, Hood's, and Polk's, the whole commanded by General Joseph Johnston, of the Confed-

crate army. I estimated the cavalry under Wheeler at
about 10,000, and the infantry and artillery at about 45,000
or 50,000 men.

To strike Dalton in front was impracticable, as it was
covered by an inaccessible ridge known as the Rocky Face,
through which was a pass between Tunnel Hill and Dalton, known as the Buzzard Roost, through which lay the
railroad and wagon-road. It was narrow, well obstructed
by abattis, and flooded by water caused by dams across
Mill Creek. Batteries also commanded it in its whole
length, from the spurs on either side, and more especially
from a ridge at the further end, like a traverse, directly
across its debouche. It was therefore necessary to turn
it. On its north front the enemy had a strong line of
works behind Mill Creek, so that my attention was at once
directed to the south. In that direction I found Snake
Creek Gap, affording me a good practicable way to reach
Resaca, a point on the enemy's railroad line of communication, eighteen (18) miles below Dalton. Accordingly I
ordered General McPherson to move rapidly from his
position at Gordon's Mill, *via* Ship's Gap, Villanow, and
Snake Creek Gap, directly on Resaca, or the railroad at
any point below Dalton, and to make a bold attack. After
breaking the railroad well, he was ordered to fall back to
a strong defensive position near Snake Creek, and stand
ready to fall upon the enemy's flank when he retreated, as
I judged he would. During the movement, General
Thomas was to make a strong feint of attack in front,
while General Schofield pressed down from the north.

General Thomas moved from Ringgold on the 7th, occupying Tunnel Hill facing the Buzzard Roost Gap, meeting with little opposition and pushing the enemy's cavalry
well through the Gap; General McPherson reached Snake

Creek Gap on the 8th, completely surprising a brigade of
cavalry, which was coming to watch and hold it; and on
the 9th General Schofield pushed down close on Dalton,
from the north, whilst General Thomas renewed his demonstration against Buzzard Roost and Rocky Faced
Ridge, pushing it almost to a battle. One division, General
Newton's, of the Fourth Corps, General Howard's, carried
the Ridge, and turning south towards Dalton, found the
crest too narrow and too well protected by rock epaul-
ments, to enable him to reach the gorge or pass. Another
division, General Geary's of the Twentieth Corps, General
Hooker's, also made a bold push for the summit, to the
south of the pass, but the narrow road as it approached
the summit was too strongly held by the enemy to be carried. This, however, was only designed as a demonstration, and worked well, for General McPherson was thereby enabled to march within a mile of Resaca almost unopposed. He found Resaca too strong to be carried by
assault, and although there were many good roads leading
from north to south, endangering his left flank from the
direction of Dalton, he could find no road by which he
could rapidly cross over to the railroad, and accordingly
he fell back and took strong position near the west end of
Snake Creek Gap. I was somewhat disappointed at the
result, still appreciated the advantage gained, and on the
10th ordered General Thomas to send General Hooker's
Corps to Snake Creek Gap in support of General McPherson,
and to follow with another corps, the Fourteenth, General
Palmer's, leaving General Howard with the Fourth Corps
to continue to threaten Dalton in front, whilst the rest of the
army moved rapidly through Snake Creek Gap. On the
same day General Schofield was ordered to follow by the
same route; and on the 11th the whole army, excepting

General Howard's corps, and some cavalry left to watch Dalton, was in motion on the west side of Rocky Faced Ridge for Snake Creek Gap and Resaca. The next day we moved against Resaca, General McPherson on the direct road, preceded by General Kilpatrick's cavalry; General Thomas to come up on his left and General Schofield on his. General Kilpatrick met and drove the enemy's cavalry from a cross-road within two miles of Resaca, but received a wound which disabled him and gave the command of his brigade to Colonel Murray, who, according to his orders, wheeled out of the road, leaving General McPherson to pass. General McPherson struck the enemy's infantry pickets near Resaca, and drove them within their fortified lines and occupied a ridge of "bald" hills, his right on the Oostanaula, about two miles below the railroad bridge, and his left abreast the town. General Thomas came up on his left, facing Camp Creek, and General Schofield broke his way through the dense forest to General Thomas's left. Johnston had left Dalton, and General Howard entered it and pressed his rear. Nothing saved Johnston's army at Resaca but the impracticable nature of the country, which made the passage of troops across the Valley almost impossible. This fact enabled his army to reach Resaca from Dalton along the comparatively good roads constructed beforehand, partly from the topographical nature of the country, and partly from the foresight of the rebel chief. At all events, on 14th of May we found the rebel army in a strong position behind Camp Creek, occupying the forts at Resaca, and his right on some high chestnut hills to the north of the town. I at once ordered a pontoon bridge to be laid across the Oostanaula at Lay's Ferry in the direction of Calhoun; a division of the Sixteenth Corps, commanded by General

Sweeney, to cross and threaten Calhoun ; also the cavalry division of General Gerrard to move from its position at Villanow down towards Rome, to cross the Oostanaula and break the railroad below Calhoun and above Kingston if possible, and with the main army I pressed against Resaca at all points. General McPherson got across Camp Creek near its mouth, and made a lodgment close up to the enemy's works, on hills that commanded, with short-range artillery, the railroad and trussel bridges ; and General Thomas pressing close along Camp Creek Valley, threw General Hooker's corps across the head of the creek to the main Dalton road, and down to it close on Resaca.

General Schofield came up close on his left, and a heavy battle ensued during the afternoon and evening of the 15th, during which General Hooker drove the enemy from several strong hills, captured a four-gun battery and many prisoners. That night, Johnston escaped, retreating south across the Oostanaula, and the next morning we entered the town in time to save the road bridge, but the railroad bridge was burned.

The whole army started in pursuit, General Thomas directly on his heels, General McPherson by Lay's Ferry, and General Schofield by obscure roads to the left. We found in Resaca another four-gun battery and a good lot of stores.

General McPherson, during the 16th, got across at Lay's Ferry. General Thomas had to make some additional bridges at Resaca, but General Schofield had more trouble, and made a wide circuit to the left by Fue's and Field's ferries across the Connasauga and Coosawattee rivers, which form the Oostanaula. On the 17th all the armies moved south by as many different roads as we could find, and General Thomas had sent by my orders a division, General Jeff. C. Davis, along the west bank of Oostanaula, to Rome. Near Adairsville we again found signs of the rebel army, and of a purpose to fight, and about sunset of that day General Newton's division, in the advance, had a pretty sharp encounter with his rear-guard; but the next morning he was gone, and we pushed on through Kingston to a point four miles beyond, where we found him again in force, on ground comparatively open, and well adapted to a grand battle. We made the proper dispositions;—General Schofield approaching Cassville from the north, to which point General Thomas had also directed General Hooker's corps; and I had drawn General McPherson's army from Woodland to Kingston, to be in close support. On the 19th the enemy was in force about Cassville, with strong forts, but as our troops converged on him, again he retreated in the night-time across the Etowah river, burning the road and railroad bridges near Cartersville, but leaving us in complete possession of the most valuable country above the Etowah river.

Holding General Thomas's army about Cassville, General McPherson's about Kingston, and General Schofield's at Cassville depot and towards the Etowah bridge, I gave the army a few days' rest, and also time to bring forward supplies for the next stage of the campaign. In the mean time, General Jeff. C. Davis had got possession of Rome with its forts, some eight or ten guns of heavy calibre, and its valuable mills and foundries. We also secured possession of two good bridges across the Etowah river, near Kingston, giving us the means of crossing towards the south. Satisfied that the enemy could and would hold us in check at the Allatoona Pass, I resolved, without even attempting it in front, to turn it by a circuit to the right,

and having supplied our wagons for twenty days' absence
from our railroad, I left a garrison at Rome and Kingston,
and on the 23d put the army in motion for "Dallas."

General McPherson crossed the Etowah at the mouth
of Conasene Creek, near Kingston, and moved for his position to the south of Dallas, *via* Van Wert. General
Davis's division moved directly from Rome for Dallas by
Van Wert. General Thomas took the road *via* Euharlee
and Burnt Hickory, while General Schofield moved by
other roads more to the east, aiming to come up on General Thomas's left.

General Thomas's head of column skirmished with the
enemy's cavalry about Burnt Hickory, and captured a
courier with a letter of General Johnston, showing that
he had detected the move and was preparing to meet us
about Dallas. The country was very rugged, mountain-
ous, and densely wooded, with few and obscure roads.

On the 25th of May, General Thomas was moving from
Burnt Hickory for Dallas, his troops on three roads, General Hooker having the advance. When he approached
the Pumpkin Vine Creek, on the main Dallas road, he
found a respectable force of the enemy's cavalry at a
bridge to his left. He rapidly pushed them across the
creek, saving the bridge though on fire, and followed out
eastward about two miles, where he first encountered infantry, whose pickets he drove some distance, until he encountered the enemy's line of battle, and his leading division, General Geary's, had a severe encounter. General
Hooker's other two divisions were on other roads, and he
ordered them in, although the road he was then following,
by reason of the presence of the enemy, led him north of
Dallas about four miles.

It was near 4 o'clock P.M. before General Hooker got

his whole corps well in hand, when he deployed two divisions, and, by my order, made a bold push to secure possession of a point known as the "New Hope" Church, where three roads meet from Ackworth, Marietta, and Dallas. Here a hard battle was fought, and the enemy was driven back to New Hope Church; but, having hastily thrown up some parapets, and a stormy, dark night having set in, General Hooker was unable to drive the enemy from those roads. By the next morning we found the enemy well intrenched, substantially in front of the road leading from Dallas to Marietta. We were consequently compelled to make dispositions on a larger scale. General McPherson was moved up to Dallas, General Thomas was deployed against New Hope Church, and General Schofield was directed towards our left, so as to strike and turn the enemy's right. General Garrard's cavalry operated with General McPherson, and General Stoneman with General Schofield. General McCook looked to our rear.

Owing to the difficult nature of the ground and dense forests, it took us several days to deploy close to the enemy, when I resolved gradually to work towards our left, and, when all things were ready, to push for the railroad east of Allatoona. In making our development before the enemy about New Hope, many severe sharp encounters occurred between parts of the army, details of which will be given at length in the reports of subordinate commanders. On the 28th, General McPherson was on the point of closing to his left on General Thomas, in front of New Hope Church, to enable me with the rest of the army to extend still more to the left and to envelop the enemy's right, when suddenly the enemy made a bold and daring assault on him at Dallas.

Fortunately our men had erected good breastworks, and gave the enemy a terrible and bloody repulse. After a few days' delay, for effect, I renewed my orders to General McPherson to move to his left about five miles, and occupy General Thomas's position in front of New Hope Church, and Generals Thomas and Schofield were ordered to move a corresponding distance to their left. This move was effected with ease and safety on the 1st of June, and, by pushing our left well around, we occupied all the roads leading back to Allatoona and Ackworth; after which I pushed General Stoneman's cavalry rapidly into Allatoona, at the east end of the Pass, and General Garrard's cavalry around by the rear to the west end of the Pass. Both of these commands reached the points designated without trouble, and we thereby accomplished our real purpose of turning the Allatoona Pass.

Ordering the railroad bridge across the Etowah to be at once rebuilt, I continued working by the left, and on the 4th of June had resolved to leave Johnston in his intrenched position at New Hope Church, and move to the railroad about Ackworth, when he abandoned his intrenchments, after which we moved readily to Ackworth and reached the railroad on the 6th of June. I at once examined in person the Allatoona Pass and found it admirably adapted to our use as a secondary base, and gave the necessary orders for its defence and garrison, and as soon as the railroad bridge was finished across the Etowah our stores came forward to our camps by rail.

At Ackworth, General Blair overtook us on the 8th of June with two divisions of the seventeenth corps that had been on furlough, and one brigade of cavalry, Colonel Long's, of General Garrard's division, which had been awaiting horses at Columbia. This accession of force about compensated for our losses in battle and the detachment left at Resaca, Rome, Kingston, and Allatoona.

On the 9th of June, our communications in the rear being secure and supplies ample, we moved forward to Big Shanty.

Kenesaw, the bold and striking Twin Mountain, lay before us, with a high range of chestnut hills trending off to the northeast, terminating to our view in another peak called Brushy Mountain. To our right was the smaller hill called Pine Mountain, and beyond it in the distance Lost Mountain. All these, though links in a continuous chain, present a sharp conical appearance, prominent in the vast landscape that presents itself from any of the hills that abound in that region. Kenesaw, Pine Mountain, and Lost Mountain form a triangle, Pine Mountain the apex, and Kenesaw and Lost Mountain the base, covering perfectly the town of Marietta and the railroad back to the Chattahoochie. On each of these peaks the enemy had his signal-stations. The summits were covered with batteries, and the spurs were alive with men, busy in felling trees, digging pits, and preparing for the grand struggle impending.

The scene was enchanting, too beautiful to be disturbed by the harsh clamors of war, but the Chattahoochie lay beyond, and I had to reach it. On approaching close to the enemy, I found him occupying a line full two miles long, more than he could hold with his force. General McPherson was ordered to move towards Marietta, his right on the railroad, General Thomas on Kenesaw and Pine Mountain, and General Schofield off towards Lost Mountain; General Garrard's cavalry on the left, General Stoneman's on the right, and General McCook looking to our rear and communications. Our depot was at Big Shanty.

By the 11th of June our lines were close up, and we made dispositions to break the line between Kenesaw and Pine mountains. General Hooker was on its right and front, General Howard on its left and front, and General Palmer between it and the railroad. During a sharp cannonading from General Howard's right or General Hooker's left, General Polk was killed on the 14th, and on the morning of the 15th Pine Mountain was found abandoned by the enemy. Generals Thomas and Schofield advanced, and found him again strongly intrenched along the line of rugged hills connecting Kenesaw and Lost mountains. At the same time General McPherson advanced his line, gaining substantial advantage on the left. Pushing our operations on the centre as vigorously as the nature of the ground would permit, I had again ordered an assault on the centre, when, on the 17th, the enemy abandoned Lost Mountain and the long line of admirable breastworks connecting it with Kenesaw. We continued to press at all points, skirmishing in dense forests of timber and across most difficult ravines, until we found him again strongly posted and intrenched, with Kenesaw as his salient, his right wing thrown back to cover Marietta, and his left behind Nose's creek, covering his railroad back to the Chattahoochie. This enabled him to contract his lines and strengthen them accordingly.

From Kenesaw he could look down upon our camps and observe every movement, and his batteries thundered away, but did us little harm, on account of the extreme height, the shot and shell passing harmlessly over our heads as we lay close up against his mountain town.

During our operations about Kenesaw the weather was villanously bad, and the rain fell almost continuously for three weeks, rendering our narrow wooded roads mere mud gulleys, so that a general movement would have been impossible; but our men daily worked closer and closer to the intrenched foe, and kept up an incessant picket firing, galling to him. Every opportunity was taken to advance our general lines closer and closer to the enemy.

General McPherson watching the enemy on Kenesaw and working his left forward, General Thomas swinging as it were on a grand left wheel, his left on Kenesaw connecting with General McPherson, and General Schofield all the time working to the south and east along the old Sandtown road. On the 22d General Hooker had advanced his line, with General Schofield on his right, the enemy, Hood's corps, with detachments from the others, suddenly sallied and attacked. The blow fell mostly on General Williams's division of General Hooker's corps, and a brigade of General Hascall's division of General Schofield's army.

The ground was comparatively open, and although the enemy drove in the skirmish lines—an advanced regiment of General Schofield, sent out purposely to hold him in check until some preparations could be completed for his reception—yet when he reached our line of battle he received a terrible repulse, leaving his dead, wounded, and many prisoners in our hands. This is known as the affair of the "Kulp House." Although inviting the enemy at all times to commit such mistakes, I could not hope for him to repeat them after the examples of Dallas and the "Kulp House," and upon studying the ground I had no alternative in my turn but to assault his lines or turn his position. Either course had its difficulties and dangers. And I perceived that the enemy and our own officers had settled down into a conviction that I would not assault fortified lines.

All looked to me to "outflank." An army to be efficient must not settle down to one single mode of offence, but must be prepared to execute any plan which promises success. I waited, therefore, for the moral effect, to make a successful assault against the enemy behind his breast-works, and resolved to attempt it at that point where success would give the largest fruits of victory. The general point selected was the left centre; because, if I could thrust a strong head of column through at that point by pushing it boldly and rapidly two and one-half miles, it would reach the railroad below Marietta, cut off the enemy's right and centre from its line of retreat, and then, by turning on either part, it could be overwhelmed and destroyed. Therefore, on the 24th of June, I ordered that an assault should be made at two points south of Kenesaw on the 27th, giving three days' notice for preparation and reconnoissance; one to be made near Little Kenesaw by General McPherson's troops, and the other about a mile further south by General Thomas's troops. The hour was fixed, and all the details given in Field Orders, No. 28, of June 24. On the 27th of June the two assaults were made at the time and in the manner prescribed, and both failed, costing us many valuable lives, among them those of Generals Harker and McCook; Colonel Rice and others badly wounded. Our aggregate loss being near 3,000, while we inflicted comparatively little loss to the enemy, who lay behind his well-formed breastworks. Failure as it was, and for which I assume the entire responsibility, I yet claim it produced good fruits, as it demonstrated to General Johnston that I would assault, and that boldly, and we also gained and held ground so close to the enemy's parapets that he could not show a head above them.

It would not do to rest long under the influence of a mistake or failure, and accordingly General Schofield was

working strong on the enemy's left; and on the 1st of July
I ordered General McPherson to be relieved by General
Garrard's cavalry in front of Kenesaw, and to rapidly
throw his whole army by the right down to and threaten
Nickajack Creek and Turner's Ferry across the Chattahoochie, and I also pushed Stoneman's cavalry to the river
below Turner's.

General McPherson commenced his movement the night
of July 2, and the effect was instantaneous. The next
morning Kenesaw was abandoned, and with the first dawn
of day I saw our skirmishers appear on the mountain-top.
General Thomas's whole line was then moved forward to
the railroad and turned south in pursuit towards the Chattahoochie. In person I entered Marietta at 8½ in the
morning, just as the enemy's cavalry vacated the place.
General Logan's corps of General McPherson's army,
which had not moved far, was ordered back into Marietta
by the main road, and General McPherson and General
Schofield were instructed to cross Nickajack and attack
the enemy in flank and rear, and, if possible, to catch him
in the confusion of crossing the Chattahoochie; but Johnston had foreseen and provided against all this, and had
covered his movement well. He had intrenched a strong
tête-du-pont at the Chattahoochie, with an advanced intrenched line across the road at Smyrna camp-meeting
ground, five miles from Marietta.

Here General Thomas found him, his front covered by a
good parapet, and his flanks behind the Nickajack and
Rottenwood creeks. Ordering a garrison for Marietta,
and General Logan to join his own army near the mouth
of Nickajack, I overtook General Thomas at Smyrna. On
the 4th of July we pushed a strong skirmish-line down
the main road, capturing the entire line of the enemy's

2

pits, and made strong demonstrations along Nickajack Creek and about Turner's Ferry. This had the desired effect, and the next morning the enemy was gone, and the army moved to the Chattahoochie, General Thomas's left flank resting on it near Paice's Ferry, General McPherson's right at the mouth of Nickajack, and General Schofield in reserve; the enemy lay behind a line of unusual strength, covering the railroad and pontoon bridges and beyond the Chattahoochie. Heavy skirmishing along our whole front during the 5th demonstrated the strength of the enemy's position, which could alone be turned by crossing the main Chattahoochie River, a rapid and deep stream, only passable at that stage by means of bridges, except at one or two very difficult fords.

To accomplish this result I judged it would be more easy of execution before the enemy had made more thorough preparation or regained full confidence, and accordingly I ordered General Schofield across from his position on the Sandtown road to Smyrna camp-ground, and next to the Chattahochie, near the mouth of Soap's Creek, and effect a lodgment on the east bank. This was most successfully and skilfully accomplished on the 7th of July, General Schofield capturing a gun, completely surprising the guard, laying a good pontoon bridge and a trestle bridge, and effecting a strong lodgment on high and commanding ground, with good roads leading to the east. At the same time General Garrard moved rapidly on Roswell and destroyed the factories which had supplied the rebel armies with cloth for years. Over one of these, the woollen-factory, the nominal owner displayed the French flag, which was not respected, of course. A neutral surely is no better than one of our own citizens, and we do not permit our own citizens to fabricate cloth for hostile uses.

General Garrard was then ordered to secure the shallow ford at Roswell, and hold it until he could be relieved by infantry; and as I contemplated transferring the Army of the Tennessee from the extreme right to the left, I ordered General Thomas to send a division of his infantry that was nearest up to Roswell to hold the ford until General Mc-Pherson could send up a corps from the neighborhood of Nickajack. General Newton's division was sent and held the ford until the arrival of General Dodge's corps, which was soon followed by General McPherson's whole army. About the same time General Howard had also built a bridge at Powers' Ferry; two miles below General Schofield had crossed over and taken a position on his right. Thus during the 9th we had secured three good and safe points of passage over the Chattahoochie, above the enemy, with good roads leading to Atlanta, and Johnston abandoned his *tête-du-pont*, burned his bridges, and left us undisputed masters north and west of the Chattahoochie, at daylight of the 10th of July.

This was one if not the chief object of the campaign, viz.: the advancement of our lines from the Tennessee to the Chattahoochie; but Atlanta lay before us only eight miles distant, and was too important a place in the hands of an enemy to be left undisturbed with its magazines, stores, arsenals, workshops, foundries, etc., and more especially its railroads, which converge there from the four great cardinal points. But the men had worked hard and needed rest, and we accordingly took a short spell. But in anticipation of this contingency I had collected a well appointed force of cavalry about 2,000 strong at Decatur, Alabama, with orders, on receiving notice by telegraph, to push rapidly south, cross the Coosa at the railroad bridge or the Ten Islands, and thence by the most direct route to

Opelika.   There is but one stem of finished railroad connecting the channels of trade and travel between Georgia,
and Alabama, and Mississippi, which runs from Montgomery
to Opelika, and my purpose was to break it up effectually,
and thereby cut off Johnston's army from that source of
supply and reinforcement.

General Rousseau, commanding the district of Tennessee,
asked permission to command the expedition, and received
it.   As soon as Johnston was well across the Chattahoochie, and as I had begun to manœuvre on Atlanta, I gave
the requisite notice, and General Rousseau started punctually on the 10th of July.   He fulfilled his orders and instructions to the very letter, whipping the rebel General
Clanton *en route;* he passed through Talladega, and
reached the railroad on the 16th about twenty-five miles
west of Opelika, and broke it well up to that place.   Also
three miles of the branch towards Columbus and two
towards West Point.   He then turned north and brought
his command safely to Marietta, arriving on the 22d, having sustained a trifling loss, not to exceed 30 men.

The main armies remained quiet in their camps on the
Chattahoochie until the 16th of July, but the time was
employed in collecting stores at Allatoona, Marietta, and
Vining's Station, strengthening the railroad guards and
garrisons, and improving the piers, bridges, and roads leading across the river.   General Stoneman's and McCook's
cavalry had scouted well down the river to draw attention
in that direction, and all things being ready for a general
advance, I ordered it to commence on the 17th; General
Thomas to cross at Powers' and Paice's Ferry bridges, and
to march by Buckhead; General Schofield was already
across at the mouth of Soap's Creek, and to march by Cross
Keys, and General McPherson to direct his course from

Roswell straight against the Augusta road, at some point east of Decatur, near Stone Mountain. General Garrard's cavalry acted with General McPherson, and Generals Stoneman and McCook watched the river and roads below the railroad. On the 17th the whole army advanced from their camps and formed a general line along the Old Peach-tree road.

Continuing on a general right-wheel, General McPherson reached the Augusta Railroad on the 18th, at a point seven miles east of Decatur, and with General Garrard's cavalry, and General Morgan L. Smith's infantry division of the Fifteenth Corps, broke up a section of about four miles, and General Schofield reached the town of Decatur.

On the 19th General McPherson turned along the railroad into Decatur, and General Schofield followed a road towards Atlanta, leading by Colonel Howard's house and the distillery, and General Thomas crossed Peach-tree Creek in force by numerous bridges in the face of the enemy's intrenched lines. All found the enemy in more or less force, and skirmished heavily.

On the 20th all the armies had closed in, converging towards Atlanta, but as a gap existed between Generals Schofield and Thomas, two divisions of General Howard's corps of General Thomas's army were moved to the left to connect with General Schofield, leaving General Newton's division of the same corps on the Buckhead road. During the afternoon of the 20th, about 4 P. M., the enemy sallied from his works in force, and fell in line of battle against our right centre, composed of General Newton's division of General Howard's corps, on the main Buckhead road; of General Hooker's corps next south, and General Johnson's division of General Palmer's corps. The blow was sudden and somewhat unexpected, but General Newton had hastily covered his front by a line of rail-piles which enabled him to meet and repulse the attack on him. General Hooker's whole corps was uncovered, and had to fight on comparatively open ground, and it, too, after a very severe battle, drove the enemy back to his intrenchments, and the action in front of General Johnston was comparatively light, that division being well intrenched. The enemy left on the field over 500 dead, about 1,000 wounded severely, 7 stands of colors, and many prisoners. His loss could not have fallen short of 5,000, whereas ours was covered by 1,500 killed, wounded, and missing; the greater loss fell on General Hooker's corps, from its exposed condition.

On the 21st we felt the enemy in his intrenched position, which was found to crown the heights overlooking the comparatively open ground of the valley of Peach-tree Creek, his right beyond the Augusta road to the east, and his left well towards Turner's Ferry on the Chattahoochie, at a general distance from Atlanta of about four miles.

On the morning of the 22d, somewhat to my surprise, this whole line was found abandoned, and I confess I thought the enemy had resolved to give us Atlanta without further contest; but General Johnston had been relieved of his command, and General Hood substituted. A new policy seemed resolved on, of which the bold attack on our right was the index. Our advancing ranks swept across the strong and well-finished parapet of the enemy, and closed in upon Atlanta, until we occupied a line in the form of a general circle of about two miles radius, when we again found him occupying in force a line of finished redoubts, which had been prepared for more than a year, covering all the roads leading into Atlanta; and we found him also busy in connecting those redoubts with curtains strengthened by rifle trenches, abattis, and chevaux-de-frise.

General McPherson, who had advanced from Decatur, continued to follow substantially the railroad, with the Fifteenth Corps, General Logan; the Seventeenth, General Blair, on its left, and the Sixteenth, General Dodge, on its right; but as the general advance of all the armies contracted the circle, the Sixteenth Corps, General Dodge, was thrown out of line by the Fifteenth connecting on the right with General Schofield, near the Howard House. General McPherson, the night before, had gained a high hill to the south and east of the railroad, where the Seventeenth Corps had, after a severe fight, driven the enemy, and it gave him a most commanding position within easy view of the very heart of the city. He had thrown out working-parties to it, and was making preparations to occupy it in strength with batteries. The Sixteenth Corps, General Dodge, was ordered from right to left to occupy this position, and make it a strong general left flank. General Dodge was moving by a diagonal path or wagon-track leading from the Decatur road in the direction of General Blair's left flank.

About 10 A. M., I was in person with General Schofield examining the appearance of the enemy's lines opposite the distillery, where we attracted enough of the enemy's fire of artillery and musketry to satisfy me the enemy was in Atlanta in force, and meant to fight, and had gone to a large dwelling close by, known as the Howard House, where General McPherson joined me. He described the condition of things on his flank, and the disposition of his troops. I explained to him that if we met serious resistance in Atlanta, as present appearances indicated, instead of operating against it by the left, I would extend to the right, and that I did not want him to gain much distance to the left. He then described the hill occupied by General Leggett's division of General Blair's corps, as essential to the occupation of any ground to the east and south of the Augusta Railroad, on account of its commanding nature. I therefore ratified his disposition of troops, and modified a previous order I had sent him in writing to use General Dodge's corps, thrown somewhat in reserve by the closing up of our line, to break up railroad, and I sanctioned its going, as already ordered by General McPherson, to his left, to hold and fortify that position. The general remained with me until near noon, when some reports reaching us that indicated a movement of the enemy on that flank, he mounted and rode away with his staff. I must here also state, that the day before I had detached General Garrard's cavalry to go to Covington, on the Augusta road, forty-two miles east of Atlanta, and from that point to send detachments to break the two important bridges across the Yellow and Ulcofauhatchee rivers, tributaries of the Ocmulgee; and General McPherson had also left his wagon-train at Decatur, under a guard of three regiments, commanded by Colonel, now General Sprague. Soon after General McPherson left me at the Howard House, as before described, I heard the sounds of musketry to our left rear; at first mere pattering shots, but soon they grew in volume, accompanied with artillery, and about the same time the sound of guns was heard in the direction of Decatur. No doubt could longer be entertained of the enemy's plan of action, which was to throw a superior force on our left flank, while he held us with his forts in front, the only question being as to the amount of force he could employ at that point. I hastily transmitted orders to all points of our centre and right to press forward and give full employment to all the enemy in his lines, and for General Schofield to hold as large a force in reserve as possible, awaiting developments. Not more than half an hour after General McPherson had left me, viz., about 12½ P. M., of the 22d, his adjutant-general, Lieutenant-Colonel Clark, rode up and reported that General McPherson was either dead or a prisoner; that he had ridden from me to General Dodge's column, moving as heretofore described, and had sent off nearly all his staff and orderlies on various errands, and himself had passed into a narrow path or road that led to the left and rear of General Giles A. Smith's division, which was General Blair's extreme left; that a few minutes after he had entered the woods a sharp volley was heard in that direction, and his horse had come out riderless, having two wounds. The suddenness of this terrible calamity would have overwhelmed me with grief, but the living demanded my whole thoughts. I instantly dispatched a staff-officer to General John A. Logan, commanding the Fifteenth Corps, to tell him what had happened; that he must assume command of the Army of the Tennessee, and hold stubbornly the ground already chosen, more especially the hill gained by General Leggett the night before.

Already the whole line was engaged in battle. Hardee's corps had sallied from Atlanta, and by a wide circuit to the east had struck General Blair's left flank, enveloped it, and his right had swung around until it hit General Dodge in motion. General Blair's line was substantially along the old line of the rebel trench, but it was fashioned to fight outwards. A space of wooded ground of near half a mile intervened between the head of General Dodge's column and General Blair's line, through which the enemy had poured, but the last order ever given by General McPher-

2*

son was to hurry a brigade (Colonel Wangelin's) of the Fifteenth Corps across from the railroad to occupy this gap. It came across on the double-quick and checked the enemy. While Hardee attacked in flank, Stewart's corps was to attack in front, directly out from the main works, but fortunately their attacks were not simultaneous. The enemy swept across the hill which our men were then fortifying, and captured the pioneer company, its tools, and almost the entire working-party, and bore down on our left until he encountered General Giles A. Smith's division of the Seventeenth Corps, who was somewhat "in air," and forced to fight first from one side of the old rifle-parapet and then from the other, gradually withdrawing regiment by regiment, so as to form a flank to General Leggett's division, which held the apex of the hill, which was the only part that was deemed essential to our future plans. General Dodge had caught and held well in check the enemy's right, and punished him severely, capturing many prisoners. Smith (General Giles A.) had gradually given up the extremity of his line and formed a new one, whose right connected with General Leggett, and his left refused, facing southeast. On this ground, and in this order, the men fought well and desperately for near four hours, checking and repulsing all the enemy's attacks. The execution on the enemy's ranks at the angle was terrible, and great credit is due both Generals Leggett and Giles A. Smith, and their men, for their hard and stubborn fighting. The enemy made no further progress on that flank, and by 4 P. M. had almost given up the attempt. In the mean time Wheeler's cavalry, unopposed (for General Garrard was absent at Covington by my order), had reached Decatur and attempted to capture the wagon-trains, but Colonel, now General Sprague, covered them with great skill

and success, sending them to the rear of Generals Schofield and Thomas, and not drawing back from Decatur
till every wagon was safe, except three which the teamsters
had left, carrying off the mules. On our extreme left the
enemy had taken a complete battery of six guns, with its
horses (Murray's), of the regular army, as it was moving
along unsupported and unapprehensive of danger, in a
narrow wooded road in that unguarded space between the
head of General Dodge's column and the line-of-battle on
the ridge above, but most of the men escaped to the bushes.
He also got two other guns on the extreme left flank, that
were left on the ground as General Giles A. Smith drew
off his men in the manner heretofore described. About
4 P. M. there was quite a lull, during which the enemy felt
forward on the railroad and main Decatur road, and suddenly assailed a regiment which, with a section of guns,
had been thrown forward as a kind of picket, and captured the two guns; he then advanced rapidly and broke
through our lines at that point which had been materially
weakened by the withdrawal of Colonel Martin's brigade,
sent by General Logan's order to the extreme left. The
other brigade, General Lightburn, which held this part of
the line, fell back in some disorder about four hundred
yards, to a position held by it the night before, leaving the
enemy for a time in possession of two batteries, one of
which, a twenty-pounder Parrott battery of four guns,
was most valuable to us, and separating General Woods'
and General Harrow's divisions of the Fifteenth Corps,
that were on the right and left of the railroad. Being in
person close by the spot, and appreciating the vast importance of the connection at that point, I ordered certain
batteries of General Schofield to be moved to a position
somewhat commanding, by a left-flank fire, and ordered an

incessant fire of shells on the enemy within sight, and the woods beyond, to prevent his reinforcing. I also sent orders to General Logan, which he had already anticipated, to make the Fifteenth Corps regain its lost ground at any cost, and instructed General Woods, supported by General Schofield, to use his division and sweep the parapet down from where he held it until he saved the batteries and recovered the lost ground. The whole was executed in superb style, at times our men and the enemy fighting across the narrow parapet; but at last the enemy gave way, and the Fifteenth Corps regained its position, and all the guns, except the two advanced ones, which were out of view and had been removed by the enemy within his main work. With this terminated the battle of the 22d, which cost us 3,722 killed, wounded, and prisoners.

But among the dead was Major-General McPherson, whose body was recovered and brought to me in the heat of battle, and I had sent it in charge of his personal staff back to Marietta, on its way to his Northern home. He was a noble youth, of striking personal appearance, of the highest professional capacity, and with a heart abounding in kindness, that drew to him the affections of all men. His sudden death devolved the command of the Army of the Tennessee on the no less brave and gallant General Logan, who nobly sustained his reputation and that of his veteran army, and avenged the death of his comrade and commander. The enemy left on the field his dead and wounded, and about a thousand well prisoners. His dead alone are computed by General Logan at 3,240, of which number 2,200 were from actual count, and of these he delivered to the enemy, under a flag of truce sent in by him (the enemy), 800 bodies. I entertain no doubt that in the battle of July 22d the enemy sustained an aggregate loss

of full 8,000 men. The next day General Garrard returned
from Covington, having succeeded perfectly in his mission,
and destroyed the bridges at Ulcofauhatchee and Yellow
rivers, besides burning a train of cars, a large quantity of
cotton (2,000 bales), and the depots of stores at Covington
and Conyer's Station, and bringing in 200 prisoners and
some good horses, losing but two men, one of whom was
killed by accident. Having, therefore, sufficiently crippled
the Augusta road, and rendered it useless to the enemy, I
then addressed myself to the task of reaching the Macon
road, over which, of necessity, came the stores and ammunition that alone maintained the rebel army in Atlanta.

Generals Schofield and Thomas had closed well up,
holding the enemy behind his inner intrenchments. I first
ordered the Army of the Tennessee to prepare to vacate its
line and to shift by the right below Proctor's Creek, and
General Schofield to extend up to the Augusta road.
About the same time General Rousseau had arrived from
his expedition to Opelika, bringing me about 2,000 good
cavalry, but of course fatigued with its long and rapid
march ; and ordering it to relieve General. Stoneman at
the river about Sandtown, I shifted General Stoneman to
our left flank, and ordered all my cavalry to prepare for a
blow at the Macon road simultaneous with the movement
of the Army of the Tennessee towards East Point. To accomplish this I gave General Stoneman the command of
his own and General Garrard's cavalry, making an effective
force of full 5,000 men ; and to General McCook I gave
his own and the new cavalry brought by General Rousseau,
which was commanded by Colonel Harrison, of the 8th
Indiana cavalry, in the aggregate about 4,000. These two
well-appointed bodies were to move in concert, the former
by the left around Atlanta to McDonough, and the latter

by the right on Fayetteville; and on a certain night, viz.,
July 28th, they were to meet on the Macon road near
Lovejoy's, and destroy it in the most effectual manner. I
estimated this joint cavalry could whip all Wheeler's
cavalry, and could otherwise fully accomplish its task; and
I think so still. I had the officers in command to meet me,
and explained the movement perfectly, and they entertained
not a doubt of perfect success. At the very moment almost
of starting, General Stoneman addressed me a note asking
permission, after fulfilling his orders and breaking the road,
to be allowed, with his command proper, to proceed to
Macon and Andersonville, and release our prisoners of war
confined at those points. There was something most cap-
tivating in the idea, and the execution was within the
bounds of probability of success. I consented that, after
the defeat of Wheeler's cavalry, which was embraced in
his orders, and breaking the road, he might attempt it with
his cavalry proper, sending that of General Garrard back
to its proper flank of the army. Both cavalry expeditions
started at the time appointed. I have as yet no report
from General Stoneman, who is a prisoner of war at Macon,
but I know that he dispatched General Garrard's cavalry
to Flat Rock, for the purpose of covering his own movement to McDonough; but for some reason unknown to me
he went off towards Covington, and did not again communicate with General Garrard at Flat Rock. General Garrard remained there until the 29th, skirmishing heavily
with a part of Wheeler's cavalry, and occupying their
attention; but hearing nothing from General Stoneman, he
moved back to Conyer's, where, learning that General
Stoneman had gone to Covington and south on the east
side of the Ocmulgee, he returned and resumed his position
on our left. It is known that General Stoneman kept to

the east of the Ocmulgee to Clinton, sending detachments
off to the east, which did a large amount of damage to the
railroad, burning the bridges of Walnut Creek and Oconee,
and destroying a large number of cars and locomotives,
and with his main force appeared before Macon. He did
not succeed in crossing the Ocmulgee at Macon, or in approaching Andersonville, but retired in the direction whence
he came, followed by various detachments of mounted men
under a General Iverson. He seems to have become
hemmed in, and gave consent to two thirds of his force to
escape back whilst he held the enemy in check with the
remainder, about 700 men, and a section of light guns.
One brigade, Colonel Adams, came in almost intact.
Another, commanded by Colonel Capron, was surprised on
the way back, and scattered; many were captured and
killed, and the balance got in mostly unarmed and afoot,
and the general himself surrendered his small command,
and is now a prisoner at Macon. His mistake was in not
making the first concentration with Generals McCook and
Garrard, near Lovejoy's, according to his orders, which is
yet unexplained.

General McCook, in the execution of his part, went
down the west bank of the Chattahoochie to near River-
town, where he laid a pontoon bridge with which he was
provided, crossed his command, and moved rapidly on
Palmetto Station of the West Point road, where he tore
up a section of track, leaving a regiment to create a diver-
sion towards Campbelltown, which regiment fulfilled its
duty, and, returned to camp by way of, and escorting back,
the pontoon-bridge train. General McCook then rapidly
moved to Fayetteville, where he found a large number of
the wagons belonging to the rebel army in Atlanta. These
he burned to the number of 500, killing 800 mules, and

carrying along others, and taking 250 prisoners, mostly
quartermasters and men belonging to the trains. He then
pushed for the railroad, reaching it at Lovejoy's Station at
the time appointed. He burned the depot, tore up a section of the road, and continued to work until forced to
leave off to defend himself against an accumulating force
of the enemy. He could hear nothing of General Stoneman, and finding his progress east too strongly opposed,
he moved south and west, and reached Newman, on the
West Point road, where he encountered an infantry force
coming from Mississippi to Atlanta, which had been stopped
by the break he had made at Palmetto. This force, with
the pursuing cavalry, hemmed him in, and forced him to
fight. He was compelled to drop his prisoners and captures,
and cut his way out, losing some 500 officers and men.
Among them a most valuable officer, Colonel Harrison,
who, when fighting his men as skirmishers on foot, was
overcome and made prisoner, and is now at Macon. He
cut his way out, reached the Chattahoochie, crossed and
got to Marietta without further loss.

General McCook is entitled to much credit for thus saving
his command, which was endangered by the failure of
General Stoneman to reach Lovejoy's. But, on the whole,
the cavalry raid is not deemed a success, for the real purpose was to break the enemy's communications, which,
though done, was on so limited a scale that I knew the
damages would soon be repaired.

Pursuant to the general plan, the Army of the Tennessee
drew out of its lines near the Decatur road during the
night of July 26, and on the 27th moved behind the rest
of the army to Proctor's Creek, and south, to prolong our
line due south, facing east. On that day, by appointment
of the President of the United States, Major-General

Howard assumed command of the Army of the Tennessee, and had the general supervision of the movement, which was made *en echelon*—General Dodge's corps, Sixteenth, on the left, nearest the enemy; General Blair's corps, Seventeenth, next to come up on its right; and General Logan's corps, Fifteenth, to come up on its right and refused as a flank; the whole to gain as much ground, due south from the flank already established on Proctor's Creek, as was consistent with a proper strength. General Dodge's men got into line in the evening of the 27th, and General Blair's came into line on his right early on the morning of the 28th, his right reaching an old meeting-house called Ezra church, near some large openfields by the Poorhouse, on a road known as the Bell's Ferry or Lickskillet road. Here the Fifteenth Corps, General Logan's, joined on and refused along a ridge well wooded, which partially commanded a view over the same fields. About 10 A. M. all the army was in position, and the men were busy in throwing up the accustomed piles of rails and logs, which after awhile assumed the form of a parapet. The skill and rapidity with which our men construct them is wonderful, and is something new in the art of war. I rode along his whole line about that time, and as I approached Ezra church there was considerable artillery firing enfilading the road in which I was riding, killing an orderly's horse just behind my staff. I struck across an open field to where General Howard was standing, in the rear of the Fifteenth Corps, and walked up to the ridge with General Morgan L. Smith, to see if the battery which enfiladed the main road and line of rail-piles could not be disposed of, and heard General Smith give the necessary orders for the deployment of one regiment forward and another to make a circuit to the right, when I returned to where General

Howard was, and remained there until 12 o'clock. During this time there was nothing to indicate serious battle, save the shelling by one or at most two batteries from beyond the large field in front of the Fifteenth Corps.

Wishing to be well prepared to defeat the enemy if he repeated his game of the 22d, I had the night before ordered General Davis's division of General Palmer's corps, which, by the movement of the Army of the Tennessee, had been left, as it were, in reserve, to move down to Turner's Ferry, and thence towards Whitehall or East Point, aiming to reach the flank of General Howard's new line, hoping that, in case of an attack, this division would in turn catch the attacking force, in flank or rear, at an unexpected moment. I explained it to General Howard, and bade him expect the arrival of such a force in case of battle. Indeed, I expected to hear the fire of its skirmishers by noon. General Davis was sick that day, and Brigadier-General Morgan commanded the division which had marched early for Turner's Ferry; but many of the roads laid down on our maps did not exist at all, and General Morgan was delayed thereby. I rode back to make more particular inquiries as to this division, and had just reached General Davis's headquarters at Proctor's Creek when I heard musketry open heavily on the right. The enemy had come out of Atlanta by the Bell's Ferry road, and formed his masses in the open fields behind a swell of ground, and, after the artillery firing I have described, advanced in parallel lines directly against the Fifteenth Corps, expecting to catch that flank in air. His advance was magnificent, but founded in an error that cost him sadly, for our men coolly and deliberately cut down his men, and, spite of the efforts of the rebel officers, his ranks broke and fled. But they were rallied again and again, as often as six times at some points, and a few of the rebel officers and men reached our lines of rail-piles only to be killed or hauled over as prisoners.

These assaults occurred from noon until about 4 P. M., when the enemy disappeared, leaving his dead and wounded in our hands. As many as 642 dead were counted and buried, and still others are known to have been buried which were not counted by the regularly detailed burial-parties.

General Logan on this occasion was conspicuous as on the 22d, his corps being chiefly engaged; but General Howard had drawn from the other corps, Sixteenth and Seventeenth, certain reserves which were near at hand, but not used. Our entire loss is reported less than 600, whereas that of the enemy, in killed and wounded, not less than 5,000. Had General Davis's division come up on the Bell's Ferry road, as I calculated, at any time before 4 o'clock, what was simply a complete repulse would have been a disastrous route to the enemy. But I cannot attribute the failure to want of energy or intelligence, and must charge it, like many other things in this campaign, to the peculiar tangled nature of the forests and absence of roads that would admit the rapid movement of troops.

This affair terminated all efforts of the enemy to check our extensions by the flank, which afterwards proceeded with comparative ease; but he met our extensions to the south by rapid and well-constructed forts and rifle-pits, built between us and the railroad to and below East Point, remaining perfectly on the defensive.

Finding that the right flank of the Army of the Tennessee did not reach, I was forced to shift General Schofield to that flank also, and afterwards General Palmer's corps of General Thomas's army. General Schofield moved from the left on the 1st of August, and General Palmer's corps followed at once, taking a line below Utoy Creek, and General Schofield prolonged it to a point near East Point. The enemy made no offensive opposition, but watched our movements, and extended his lines and parapets accordingly.

About this time several changes in important commands occurred, which should be noted. General Hooker, offended that General Howard was preferred to him as the successor of General McPherson, resigned his command of the Twentieth Corps, to which General Slocum was appointed; but he was at Vicksburg, and, until he joined, the command of the corps devolved on General H. S. Williams, who handled it admirably. General Palmer also resigned the command of the Fourteenth Corps, and General Jeff. C. Davis was appointed to his place. Major-General D. S. Stanley had succeeded General Howard in the command of the Fourth Corps.

From the 2d to the 5th we continued to extend to the right, demonstrating strongly on the left and along our whole line. General Reilley's brigade of General Cox's division, General Schofield's army, on the 5th tried to break through the enemy's line about a mile below Utoy Creek, but failed to carry the position, losing about 400 men, who were caught in the entanglements and abattis; but the next day the position was turned by General Hascall, and General Schofield advanced his whole line close up to and facing the enemy below Utoy Creek. Still he did not gain the desired foothold on either the West Point or Macon railroad. The enemy's line at that time must have been near fifteen miles long, extending from near Decatur to below East Point. This he was enabled to do by the use of a large force of State militia, and his position was so masked by the shape of the ground that we were unable to discover the weak parts.

I had become satisfied that to reach the Macon road, and thereby control the supplies for Atlanta, I would have to move the whole army; but before beginning, I ordered down from Chattanooga four four-and-a-half-inch rifled guns, to try their effect. These arrived on the 10th, and were put to work night and day, and did execution on the city, causing frequent fires, and creating confusion; yet the enemy seemed determined to hold his forts, even if the city were destroyed. On the 16th of August I made my orders, No. 57, prescribing the mode and manner of executing the grand movement by the right flank, to begin on the 18th. This movement contemplated the withdrawal of the Twentieth Corps, General Williams, to the intrenched position at the Chattahoochie Bridge, and the march of the main army to the West Point Railroad, near Fairborn, and afterwards to the Macon road, at or near Jonesboro', with our wagons loaded with provisions for fifteen days. About the time of the publication of these orders I learned that Wheeler, with a large mounted force of the enemy, variously estimated from 6,000 to 10,000 men, had passed around by the east and north, and had made his appearance on our lines of communication near Adairsville, and had succeeded in capturing 900 of our beef-cattle, and had made a break of the railroad near Calhoun. I could not have asked any thing better, for I had provided well against such a contingency, and this detachment left me superior to the enemy in cavalry. I suspended the execution of my orders for the time being, and ordered General Kilpatrick to make up a well-appointed force of about 5,000 cavalry, and to move from his camp about Sandtown, during the night of the 18th, to the West Point road, and break it good near Fairborn; then to proceed across to the Macon road, and tear it up thoroughly; to avoid as far as possible the enemy's infantry, but to attack any cavalry he could find. I thought this cavalry would save the necessity or moving the main army across, and that, in case of his success, it would leave me in better position to take full advantage of the result.

General Kilpatrick got off at the time appointed, and broke the West road, and afterwards reached the Macon road at Jonesboro', where he whipped Ross's cavalry and got possession of the railroad, which he held for five hours, damaging it considerably. But a brigade of the enemy's infantry, which had been dispatched below Jonesboro' in cars, was run back and disembarked, and, with Jackson's rebel cavalry, made it impossible for him to continue his work. He drew off to the east, and made a circuit, and struck the railroad about Lovejoy's Station, but was again threatened by the enemy, who moved on shorter lines, when he charged through their cavalry, taking many prisoners, of which he brought in 70, and captured a four-gun battery, which he destroyed, except one gun, which he brought in. He estimated the damage done to the road as enough to interrupt its use for ten days; after which he returned by a circuit north and east, reaching Decatur on the 22d. After an interview with General Kilpatrick, I was satisfied that whatever damage he had done would not produce the result desired, and I renewed my orders for the movement of the whole army. This involved the necessity of raising the siege of Atlanta, taking the field with our main force, and using it against the communications of Atlanta instead of against its intrenchments. All the army commanders were at once notified to send their surplus wagons, encumbrances of all kinds, and sick, back to our intrenched position at the bridge, and that the movement would begin during the night of the 25th. Accordingly, all things being ready, the Fourth Corps, General Stanley, drew out of its lines on our extreme left, and marched to a position below Proctor's Creek. The Twentieth Corps, General Williams, moved back to the Chattahoochie. This movement was made without loss, save a few things left in our camps by thoughtless officers or men. The night of the 26th the movement continued, the Army of the Tennessee drawing out and moving rapidly by a circuit well towards Sandtown and across Camp Creek, the Army of the Cumberland below Utoy Creek, General Schofield, remaining in position. This was effected with the loss of but a single man in the Army of the Tennessee, wounded by a shell from the enemy. The third movement brought the Army of the Tennessee on the West Point Railroad, above Fairborn, the Army of the Cumberland about Red Oak, and General Schofield closed in near Digs and Mins. I then ordered one day's work to be expended in destroying that road, and it was done with a will. Twelve and one-half miles were destroyed, the ties burned, and the iron rails heated and tortured by the utmost ingenuity of old hands at the work. Several cuts were filled up with the trunks of trees, with logs, rock, and earth intermingled with loaded shells, prepared as torpedoes, to explode in case of an attempt to clear them out. Having personally inspected this work, and satisfied with its execution, I ordered the whole army to move the next day eastward by several roads: General Howard on the right, towards Jonesboro'; General Thomas, the centre, by Shoal Creek church to Couch's, on the Decatur and Fayetteville road; and General Schofield on the left, about Morrow's mills. An inspection of the map will show the strategic advantages of this position. The railroad from Atlanta to Macon follows substantially the ridge or " divide" between the waters of Flint and Ocmulgee rivers, and from east Point to Jonesboro' makes a wide bend to the east. Therefore the position I have described, which had been well studied on paper, was my first " objective." It gave me " interior lines," something our enemy had enjoyed too long, and I was anxious for once to get the inside track, and therefore my haste and desire to secure it.

The several columns moved punctually on the morning of the 29th. General Thomas, on the centre, encountered little opposition or difficulty, save what resulted from the narrow roads, and reached his position at Couch's early in the afternoon ; General Schofield being closer to the enemy, who still clung to East Point, moved cautiously on a small circle around that point, and came into position towards Rough-and-Ready ; and General Howard, having the outer circle, had a greater distance to move. He encountered cavalry, which he drove rapidly to the crossing of Shoal Creek, where the enemy also had artillery. Here a short delay occurred, and some cannonading and skirmishing ; but General Howard started them again, and kept them moving, passed the Renfro place on the Decatur road, which was the point indicated for him in the orders of that day ; but he wisely and well kept on, and pushed on towards Jonesboro', saved the bridge across Flint River, and did not halt until darkness compelled him, within half a mile of Jonesboro'. Here he rested for the night, and on the morning of August 31st, finding himself in the presence of a heavy force of the enemy, he deployed the Fifteenth Corps, and disposed the Sixteenth and Seventeenth on its flanks. The men covered their front with the usual parapet, and were soon prepared to act offensively or

defensively, as the case called for. I was that night with
General Thomas at Couch's, and as soon as I learned that
General Howard had passed Renfro's, I directed General
Thomas to send to that place a division of General Jeff.
C. Davis's corps, to move General Stanley's corps, in connection with General Schofield's, towards Rough-and-
Ready, and then to send forward due east a strong detachment of General Davis's corps, to feel for the railroad.
General Schofield was also ordered to move boldly forward
and strike the railroad near Rough-and-Ready. These
movements were progressing during the 31st, when the
enemy came out of his works at Jonesboro', and attacked
General Howard in position described. General Howard
was admirably situated to receive him, and repulse the
attack thoroughly. The enemy attacked with Lee's and
Hardee's corps, and after a contest of over two hours
withdrew, leaving over 400 dead on the ground; and his
wounded, of which about 300 were left in Jonesboro',
could not have been less than 2,500. Hearing the sounds
of battle at Jonesboro' about noon, orders were renewed
to push the other movements on the left and centre, and
about 4 P. M. the reports arrived simultaneously that General Howard had thoroughly repulsed the enemy at Jonesboro'; that General Schofield had reached the railroad a
mile below Rough-and-Ready, and was working up the
road, breaking it as he went; that General Stanley, of
General Thomas's army, had also got the road below General Schofield, and was destroying its working south; and
that General Baird, of General Davis's corps, had struck it
still lower down, within four miles of Jonesboro'.

Orders were at once given for all the army to turn on
Jonesboro', General Howard to keep the enemy busy
whilst General Thomas should move down from the north,

3

with General Schofield on his left. I also ordered the troops, as they moved down, to continue the thorough de-struction of the railroad, because we had it then, and I did not know but that events might divert our attention. General Garrard's cavalry was directed to watch the roads to our rear, the north. General Kilpatrick was sent south, down the west bank of Flint, with instructions to attack or threaten the railroad below Jonesboro'. I expected the whole army would close down on Jonesboro' by noon of the 1st of September. General Davis's corps, having a shorter distance to travel, was on time and deployed, facing south, his right in connection with General Howard, and his left on the railroad. General Stanley and General Schofield were coming down along the Rough-and-Ready road, and along the railroad, breaking it as they came. When General Davis joined to General Howard, General Blair's corps on General Howard's left was thrown in re-serve, and was immediately sent well to the right below Jonesboro' to act against the flank along with General Kilpatrick's cavalry. About 4 P. M. General Davis was all ready, and assaulted the enemy's lines across open fields, carrying them very handsomely, and taking as prisoners the greater part of Govan's brigade, including its com-mander, with two four-gun batteries. Repeated orders were sent to Generals Stanley and Schofield to hurry up, but the difficult nature of the country and the absence of roads are the reasons assigned why these troops did not get well into position for attack before night rendered fur-ther operations impossible. Of course, the next morning the enemy was gone, and had retreated south. About 2 o'clock that night, the sounds of heavy explosions were heard in the direction of Atlanta, distance about twenty miles, with a succession of minor explosions, and what

seemed like the rapid firing of cannon and musketry.
These continued for about an hour, and again, about 4
A. M., occurred another series of similar discharges, ap-
parently nearer us, and these sounds could be accounted
for on no other hypothesis than of a night attack on Atlanta by General Slocum, or the blowing up of the enemy's
magazines. Nevertheless, at daybreak, on finding the
enemy gone from his lines at Jonesboro', I ordered a general pursuit south, General Thomas following to the left of
the railroad, General Howard on his right, and General
Schofield keeping off about two miles to the east. We
overtook the enemy again, near Lovejoy's Station, in a
strong intrenched position, with his flanks well protected
behind a branch of Walnut Creek, to the right, and a con-
fluent of the Flint River to his left. We pushed close up
and reconnoitred the ground, and found he had evidently
halted to cover his communication with the McDonough
and Fayetteville road.

Rumors began to arrive, through prisoners captured,
that Atlanta had been abandoned during the night of September 1st, that Hood had blown up his ammunition trains,
which accounted for the sounds so plainly heard by us, and
which were yet unexplained; that Stewart's corps was
then retreating towards McDonough, and that the militia
had gone off towards Covington. It was then too late to
interpose and prevent their escape, and I was satisfied
with the substantial success already gained. Accordingly,
I ordered the work of destroying railroad to cease, and
the troops to be held in hand ready for any movement that
further information from Atlanta might warrant.

General Jeff. C. Davis's corps had been left above Jonesboro', and General Garrard's cavalry was still further back,
and the latter was ordered to send back to Atlanta and

ascertain the exact truth and the real situation of affairs.
But the same night, viz., of September 4th, a courier arrived from General Slocum reporting the fact that the
enemy had evacuated Atlanta, blown up seven trains of
cars, and had retreated on the McDonough road. General
Slocum had entered and taken possession on the 2d of
September.

The object of my movement against the railroad was
therefore already reached and concluded, and as it was
idle to pursue our enemy in that wooded country, with a
view to his capture, I gave orders on the 4th for the army
to prepare to move back slowly to Atlanta. On the 5th
we drew back to the vicinity of Jonesboro', five miles,
where we remained a day. On the 7th we moved to
Rough-and Ready, seven miles, and the next day to the
camps selected, viz.: the Army of the Cumberland grouped round about Atlanta, the Army of the Tennessee about
East Point, and that of the Ohio at Decatur, where the
men now occupy clean and healthy camps.

I have not yet received full or satisfactory accounts of
Wheeler's operations to our rear, further than that he
broke the road about Calhoun, and then made his appearance at Dalton, where Colonel Laibold held him in check
until General Steedman arrived from Chattanooga and
drove him off. He then passed up into East Tennessee,
and made quite a stay at Athens; but, on the first show
of pursuit, he kept on north across the Little Tennessee;
and crossing the Holston near Strawberry Plains, reached
the Clinch near Clinton, and passed over towards Sequatchee and McMinnville. Thence he seems to have gone to
Murfreesboro' and Lebanon, and across to Franklin. He
may have committed damage to the property of citizens,
but has injured us but little, the railroads being repaired

about as fast as he broke them. From Franklin he has been pursued towards Florence, and out of the State by Generals Rousseau, Steedman, and Granger; but what amount of execution they have done to him is not yet reported. Our roads and telegraph are all repaired, and the cars run with regularity and speed. It is proper to remark in this place, that during the operations of this campaign expeditions were sent out from Memphis and Vicksburg to check any movements of the enemy's forces in Mississippi upon our communications. The manner in which this object was accomplished reflects credit upon Generals A. J. Smith, Washburne, Slocum, and Mower; and although General Sturgis's expedition was less successful than the others, it assisted us in the main object to be accomplished.

I must bear full and liberal testimony to the energetic and successful management of our railroads during the campaign. No matter when or where a break has been made, the repair-train seemed on the spot, and the damage was repaired generally before I knew of the break. Bridges have been built with surprising rapidity, and the locomotive whistle was heard in our advanced camps almost before the echoes of the skirmish fire had ceased. Some of these bridges—those of the Oostanaula, the Etowah, and Chattahoochie—are fine, substantial structures, and were built in inconceivably short time, almost out of material improvised on the spot.

Colonel W. W. Wright, who has charge of the "construction and repairs," is not only a most skilful, but a wonderfully ingenious, industrious, and zealous officer, and I can hardly do him justice. In like manner the officers charged with running the trains have succeeded to my entire satisfaction, and have worked in perfect harmony with the quartermasters and commissaries, bringing forward abundant supplies with such regularity that at no one time have we wanted for provisions, forage, ammunition, or stores of any essential kind.

Colonel L. C. Easton, chief quartermaster, and Colonel A. Beckwith, chief commissary, have also succeeded, in a manner surprising to all of us, in getting forward supplies. I doubt if ever an army was better supplied than this, and I commend them most highly for it, because I know that more solicitude was felt by the lieutenant-general commanding, and by the military world at large, on this than on any other one problem involved in the success of the campaign.

Captain T. G. Baylor, chief ordnance officer, has in like manner kept the army well supplied at all times with every kind of ammunition. To Captain O. M. Poe, chief engineer, I am more than ordinarily indebted for keeping me supplied with maps and information of roads, and topography, as well as in the more important branch of his duties in selecting lines and military positions. My own personal staff has been small, but select.

Brigadier-General W. F. Barry, an officer of enlarged capacity and great experience, has filled the office of chief of artillery to perfection; and Lieutenant-Colonel E. D. Kitto, chief medical inspector, has done every thing possible to give proper aid and direction to the operations of that important department. I have never seen the wounded removed from the fields of battle, cared for, and afterwards sent to proper hospitals in the rear, with more promptness, system, care, and success, than during this whole campaign, covering over one hundred days of actual battle and skirmish.

My aides-de-camp, Major J. C. McCoy, Captain L. M. Dayton, and Captain J. C. Audenried have been ever zealous and most efficient, carrying my orders day and night to distant points of our extended lines, with an intelligence and zeal that insured the perfect working of machinery, covering from ten to twenty-five miles of ground, when the least error in the delivery and explanation of an order would have produced confusion; whereas in great measure, owing to the intelligence of these officers, orders have been made so clear that these vast armies have moved side by side, sometimes crossing each other's tracks through a difficult country of over a hundred and thirty-eight miles in length, without confusion or trouble.

Captain Dayton has also fulfilled the duties of my adjutant-general, making all orders and carrying on the official correspondence.

Three inspectors-general completed my staff: Brigadier-General J. M. Corse, who has since been assigned the command of a division of the Sixteenth Corps, at the request of General Dodge; Lieutenant-Colonel W. Warner, of the 76th Ohio, and Lieutenant-Colonel Charles Ewing, inspector-general of the Fifteenth Corps and captain 13th United States Regulars.

These officers, of singular energy and intelligence, have been of immense assistance to me in handling these large armies.

My three "armies in the field" were commanded by able officers, my equals in rank and experience: Major-General George H. Thomas, Major-General J. M. Schofield, and Major-General O. O. Howard. With such commanders, I had only to indicate the object desired, and they accomplished it. I cannot over-estimate their services to the country, and must express my deep and heartfelt thanks that, coming together from different fields, with different interests, they have co-operated with a harmony that has been productive of the greatest amount of success and good feeling. A more harmonious army does not exist.

I now inclose their reports, and those of the corps, division, and brigade commanders, a perusal of which will fill up the sketch which I have endeavored to make. I also submit tabular statements of our losses in battle by wounds and sickness; also, lists of prisoners captured, sent to the rear, and exchanged; also, of the guns and materials of war captured, besides the important country, towns, and arsenals of the enemy that we now "occupy and hold."

All of which is respectfully submitted,

W. T. SHERMAN, Major-General Commanding.

Major-General H. W. HALLECK,
   Chief of Staff, Washington, D. C.

General Sherman issued an order, September 4th, to the effect that the city of Atlanta being exclusively required for warlike purposes, all citizens must remove from it; and to expedite such removal, he entered into a truce with General Hood, and made arrangements with him for forwarding the citizens and their effects beyond the Federal lines. In connection with this event the following correspondence took place between the authorities of Atlanta and General Sherman.

ATLANTA, Ga., Sept. 11, 1864.

MAJOR-GENERAL W. T. SHERMAN—*Sir:* The undersigned, Mayor and two members of Council for the city of Atlanta, for the time being the only legal organ of the people of said city to express their wants and wishes, ask leave most earnestly, but respectfully, to petition you to reconsider the order requiring them to leave Atlanta. At

first view it struck us that the measure would involve extraordinary hardship and loss, but since we have seen the
practical execution of it, so far as it has progressed, and
the individual condition of many of the people, and heard
the statements as to the inconveniences, loss, and suffering
attending it, we are satisfied that the amount of it will involve in the aggregate consequences appalling and heart-
rending.

Many poor women are in an advanced state of preg-
nancy; others having young children, whose husbands, for
the greater part, are either in the army, prisoners, or dead.
Some say: "I have such a one sick at my house; who
will wait on them when I am gone?" Others say: "What
are we to do? we have no houses to go to, and no means
to buy, build, or rent any; no parents, relatives, or friends
to go to." Another says: "I will try and take this or
that article of property; but such and such things I must
leave behind, though I need them much." We reply to
them: "General Sherman will carry your property to
Rough-and-Ready, and then General Hood will take it
thence on." And they will reply to that: "But I want to
leave the railroad at such a place, and cannot get convey-
ance from thence on."

We only refer to a few facts to illustrate, in part, how
this measure will operate in practice. As you advanced,
the people north of us fell back, and before your arrival
here a large portion of the people had retired south;
so that the country south of this is already crowded, and
without sufficient houses to accommodate the people, and
we are informed that many are now staying in churches
and other outbuildings. This being so, how is it possible for the people still here (mostly women and children)
to find shelter, and how can they live through the winter

3*

in the woods—no shelter or subsistence—in the midst of strangers who know them not, and without the power to assist them much if they were willing to do so?

This is but a feeble picture of the consequences of this measure. You know the woe, the horror, and the suffering cannot be described by words. Imagination can only conceive of it, and we ask you to take these things into consideration. We know your mind and time are continually occupied with the duties of your command, which almost deters us from asking your attention to the matter, but thought it might be that you had not considered the subject in all of its awful consequences, and that, on reflection, you, we hope, would not make this people an exception to all mankind, for we know of no such instance ever having occurred—surely not in the United States. And what has this helpless people done that they should be driven from their homes, to wander as strangers, outcasts, and exiles, and to subsist on charity?

We do not know as yet the number of people still here. Of those who are here, a respectable number, if allowed to remain at home, could subsist for several months without assistance; and a respectable number for a much longer time, and who might not need assistance at any time.

In conclusion, we most earnestly and solemnly petition you to reconsider this order, or modify it, and suffer this unfortunate people to remain at home and enjoy what little means they have.

Respectfully submitted,

JAMES M. CALHOUN, Mayor.

E. E. RAWSON, S. C. WELLS, Councilmen.

HEADQUARTERS MILITARY DIVISION OF THE MISSISSIPPI,
In the Field, Atlanta, Ga., Sept. 12, 1864.

JAMES M. CALHOUN, *Mayor*, E. E. RAWSON *and* S.'C. WELLS, *representing City Council of Atlanta.*

GENTLEMEN—I have your letter of the 11th, in the nature of a petition to revoke my orders removing all the inhabitants from Atlanta. I have read it carefully, and give full credit to your statements of the distress that will be occasioned by it, and yet shall not revoke my order, simply because my orders are not designed to meet the humanities of the case, but to prepare for the future struggles in which millions, yea hundreds of millions of good people outside of Atlanta have a deep interest. We must have *Peace*, not only at Atlanta, but in all America. To secure this, we must stop the war that now desolates our once happy and favored country. To stop war, we must defeat the rebel armies that are arrayed against the laws and Constitution which all must respect and obey. To defeat these armies, we must prepare the way to reach them in their recesses, provided with the arms and instruments which enable us to accomplish our purpose.

Now I know the vindictive nature of our enemy, and that we may have many years of military operations from this quarter, and therefore deem it wise and prudent to prepare in time. The use of Atlanta for warlike purposes is inconsistent with its character as a home for families. There will be no manufactures, commerce, or agriculture here for the maintenance of families, and sooner or later want will compel the inhabitants to go. Why not go *now*, when all the arrangements are completed for the transfer, instead of waiting till the plunging shot of contending armies will renew the scene of the past month? Of course I do not apprehend any such thing at this moment, but you do not suppose that this army will be here till the war is over. I cannot discuss this subject with you fairly, because I cannot impart to you what I propose to do, but I assert that my military plans make it necessary for the inhabitants to go away, and I can only renew my offer of services to make their exodus in any direction as easy and comfortable as possible. You cannot qualify war in harsher terms than I will.

War is cruelty, and you cannot refine it; and those who brought war on the country deserve all the curses and maledictions a people can pour out. I know I had no hand in making this war, and I know I will make more sacrifices to-day than any of you to secure peace. But you cannot have peace and a division of our country. If the United States submits to a division now, it will not stop, but will go on till we reap the fate of Mexico, which is eternal war. The United States does and must assert its authority wherever it has power; if it relaxes one bit to pressure it is gone, and I know that such is not the national feeling. This feeling assumes various shapes, but always comes back to that of *Union*. Once admit the Union, once more acknowledge the authority of the national Government, and instead of devoting your houses, and streets, and roads to the dread uses of war, I, and this army, become at once your protectors and supporters, shielding you from danger, let it come from what quarter it may. I know that a few individuals cannot resist a torrent of error and passion such as has swept the South into rebellion; but you can point out, so that we may know those who desire a Government and those who insist on war and its desolation.

You might as well appeal against the thunder-storm as against these terrible hardships of war. They are inevitable, and the only way the people of Atlanta can hope once more to live in peace and quiet at home is to stop this war, which can alone be done by admitting that it began in error and is perpetuated in pride. We don't want your negroes or your horses, or your houses or your land, or any thing you have; but we do want and will have a just obedience to the laws of the United States. That we will have, and if it involves the destruction of your improvements, we cannot help it. You have heretofore read public sentiment in your newspapers, that live by falsehood and excitement, and the quicker you seek for truth in other quarters the better for you.

I repeat, then, that, by the original compact of the Government, the United States had certain rights in Georgia which have never been relinquished, and never will be; that the South began war by seizing forts, arsenals, mints, custom-houses, etc., etc., long before Mr. Lincoln was installed, and before the South had one jot or tittle of provocation. I myself have seen in Missouri, Kentucky, Tennessee, and Mississippi, hundreds and thousands of women and children fleeing from your armies and desperadoes, hungry and with bleeding feet. In Memphis, Vicksburg, and Mississippi we fed thousands upon thousands of the families of rebel soldiers left on our hands, and whom we could not see starve. Now that war comes home to you, you feel very different—you deprecate its horrors, but did not feel them when you sent car-loads of soldiers, and ammunition, and moulded shell and shot to carry war into Kentucky and Tennessee, and desolate the homes of hundreds and thousands of good people, who only asked to live in peace at their old homes, and under the Government of their inheritance. But these comparisons are idle. I want peace, and believe it can only be reached through

Union and war, and I will ever conduct war purely with a view to perfect and early success.

But, my dear sirs, when that peace does come, you may call on me for any thing. Then will I share with you the last cracker, and watch with you to shield your homes and families against dangers from every quarter. Now you must go, and take with you the old and feeble; feed and nurse them, and build for them in more quiet places proper habitations to shield them against the weather, until the mad passions of men cool down, and allow the Union and peace once more to settle on your old homes at Atlanta.

Yours, in haste,

W. T. SHERMAN, Major-General.

ATLANTA, Ga., Sept. 20, 1864.

ON leaving Atlanta, I should return my thanks to General Sherman, General Slocum, General Ward, Colonel Colburn, Major Peck, Captain Mott, Captain Stewart, Captain Flagg, and all the other officers with whom I have had business transactions in carrying out the order of General Sherman for the removal of the citizens, and in transacting my private business; for their kindness and their patience in answering the many inquiries I had to make on the duration of the delicate and arduous duties devolving on me as Mayor of this city.

Respectfully,

JAS. M. CALHOUN.

II.

FROM ATLANTA TO SAVANNAH,

THROUGH THE HEART OF GEORGIA.

HEADQUARTERS MILITARY DIVISION OF THE MISSISSIPPI,
In the Field, Savannah, Ga., January 1, 1865.

Major-General H. W. HALLECK, *Chief of Staff, Washington City, D. C.*

GENERAL—I have the honor to offer my report of the operations of the armies under my command since the occupation of Atlanta, in the early part of September last, up to the present date.

As heretofore reported, in the month of September, the Army of the Cumberland, Major-General Thomas commanding, held the city of Atlanta; the Army of the Tennessee, Major-General Howard commanding, was grouped about East Point; and the Army of the Ohio, Major-General Schofield commanding, held Decatur. Many changes occurred in the composition of those armies, in consequence of the expiration of the time of service of many of the regiments. The opportunity was given to us to consolidate the fragments, re-clothe and equip the men, and make preparations for the future campaign. I also availed myself of the occasion to strengthen the garrisons to our rear, to make our communications more secure, and sent Wagner's division of the Fourth Corps and Morgan's division of the Fourteenth Corps back to Chattanooga, and Corse's division of the Fifteenth Corps to Rome. Also a thorough reconnoissance was made of Atlanta, and a new line of works begun, which required a small garrison to hold.

During this month the enemy, whom we had left at Lovejoy's Station, moved westward towards the Chattahoochie, taking position facing us, and covering the West Point Railroad, about Palmetto Station. He also threw a pontoon bridge across the Chattahoochie, and sent cavalry detachments to the west, in the direction of Carrolton and Powder Springs. About the same time President Davis visited Macon, and his army at Palmetto, and made harangues referring to an active campaign against us. Hood still remained in command of the Confederate forces, with Cheatham, S. D. Lee, and Stewart, commanding his three corps, and Wheeler in command of his cavalry, which had been largely re-enforced.

My cavalry consisted of two divisions. One was stationed at Decatur, under command of Brigadier-General Garrard; the other, commanded by Brigadier-General Kilpatrick, was posted near Sandtown, with a pontoon bridge over the Chattahoochie, from which he could watch any movement of the enemy towards the west.

As soon as I became convinced that the enemy intended to assume the offensive, namely, September 28, I sent Major-General Thomas, second in command, to Nashville, to organize the new troops expected to arrive, and to make preliminary preparations to meet such an event.

About the 1st of October some of the enemy's cavalry made their appearance on the west of the Chattahoochie, and one of his infantry corps was reported near Powder Springs, and I received authentic intelligence that the rest of his infantry was crossing to the west of the Chattahoochie. I at once made my orders that Atlanta and the Chattahoochie railroad-bridge should be held by the Twentieth Corps, Major-General Slocum; and on the 4th of October put in motion the Fifteenth and Seventeenth

Corps, and the Fourth, Fourteenth, and Twenty-third Corps, to Smyrna camp-ground, and on the 5th moved to the strong position about Kenesaw. The enemy's cavalry had, by a rapid movement, got upon our railroad at Big Shanty, and broken the line of telegraph and railroad, and, with a division of infantry (French's), had moved against Allatoona, where were stored about a million of rations. Its redoubts were garrisoned by three small regiments under Colonel Tourtellotte, 4th Minnesota.

I had anticipated this movement, and had, by signal and telegraph, ordered General Corse to re-enforce that post from Rome. General Corse had reached Allatoona with a brigade during the night of the 4th, just in time to meet the attack by French's division on the morning of the 5th. In person I reached Kenesaw Mountain about 10 A. M. of the 5th, and could see the smoke of battle and hear the faint sounds of artillery. The distance, eighteen miles, was too great for me to make in time to share in the battle, but I directed the Twenty-third Corps, Brigadier-General Cox commanding, to move rapidly from the base of Kenesaw due west, aiming to reach the road from Allatoona to Dallas, threatening the rear of the forces attacking Allatoona. I succeeded in getting a signal message to General Corse during his fight, notifying him of my presence. The defence of Allatoona by General Corse was admirably conducted, and the enemy repulsed with heavy slaughter. His description of the defence is so graphic that it leaves nothing for me to add; and the movement of General Cox had the desired effect of causing the withdrawal of French's division rapidly in the direction of Dallas.

On the 6th and 7th I pushed my cavalry well towards Burnt Hickory and Dallas, and discovered that the enemy had moved westward, and inferred that he would attempt to break our railroad again in the neighborhood of Kingston. Accordingly, on the morning of the 8th, I put the army in motion through Allatoona Pass to Kingston, reaching that point on the 10th. There I learned that the enemy had feigned on Rome, and was passing the Coosa River on a pontoon bridge about eleven miles below Rome. I therefore, on the 11th, moved to Rome, and pushed Garrard's cavalry and the Twenty-third Corps, under General Cox, across the Oostenaula, to threaten the flanks of the enemy passing north. Garrard's cavalry drove a cavalry brigade of the enemy to and beyond the Narrows, leading into the valley of the Chattooga, capturing two field-pieces. The enemy had moved with great rapidity, and made his appearance at Resaca, and Hood had in person demanded its surrender.

I had from Kingston re-enforced Resaca by two regiments of the Army of the Tennessee. I at first intended to move the army into the Chattooga Valley, to interpose between the enemy and his line of retreat down the Coosa, but feared that General Hood would in that event turn eastward by Spring Place, and down the Federal road, and therefore moved against him at Resaca. Colonel Weaver at Resaca, afterwards re-enforced by General Raum's brigade, had repulsed the enemy from Resaca; but he had succeeded in breaking the railroad from Filton to Dalton, and as far north as the tunnel. Arriving at Resaca on the evening of the 14th, I determined to strike Hood in flank, or force him to battle, and directed the Army of the Tennessee, General Howard, to move to Snake Creek Gap, which was held by the enemy, while General Stanley, with the Fourth and Fourteenth Corps, moved by Tilton across the mountains to the rear of Snake Creek Gap, in the neighborhood of Villanow.

The Army of the Tennessee found the enemy occupying our old lines in Snake Creek Gap, and on the 15th skirmished for the purpose of holding him there until Stanley could get to his rear. But the enemy gave way about noon, and was followed through the Gap, escaping before General Stanley had reached the further end of the pass. The next day (the 16th) the armies moved directly towards Lafayette, with a view to cut off Hood's retreat. We found him intrenched in Ship's Gap, but the leading division (Wood's) of the Fifteenth Corps rapidly carried the advanced posts held by two companies of a South Carolina regiment, making them prisoners. The remaining eight companies escaped to the main body near Lafayette. The next morning we passed over into the valley of the Chattooga, the Army of the Tennessee moving in pursuit by Lafayette and Alpine towards Blue Pond; the Army of the Cumberland by Summerville and Melville post-office to Gaylesville; and the Army of the Ohio and Garrard's cavalry from Villanow, Dirttown, and Gover's Gap to Gaylesville. Hood, however, was little encumbered with trains, and marched with great rapidity, and had succeeded in getting into the narrow gorge formed by the Lookout range abutting against the Coosa River in the neighborhood of Gadsden. He evidently wanted to avoid a fight.

On the 19th all the armies were grouped about Gaylesville, in the rich valley of the Chattooga, abounding in corn and meat, and I determined to pause in my pursuit of the enemy, to watch his movements and live on the country. I hoped that Hood would turn towards Guntersville and Bridgeport. The Army of the Tennessee was posted near Little River, with instructions to feel forward in support of the cavalry, which was ordered to watch Hood in the neighborhood of Will's Valley, and to give me the earliest notice possible of his turning northward. The Army of the Ohio was posted at Cedar Bluff, with orders to lay a pontoon across the Coosa, and to feel forward to Centre and down in the direction of Blue Mountain. The Army of the Cumberland was held in reserve at Gaylesville ; and all the troops were instructed to draw heavily for supplies from the surrounding country. In the mean time communications were opened to Rome, and a heavy force set to work in repairing the damages done to our railroads. Atlanta was abundantly supplied with provisions, but forage was scarce, and General Slocum was instructed to send strong foraging-parties out in the direction of South River, and collect all the corn and fodder possible, and to put his own trains in good condition for further service.

Hood's movements and strategy had demonstrated that he had an army capable of endangering at all times my communications, but unable to meet me in open fight. To follow him would simply amount to being decoyed away from Georgia, with little prospect of overtaking and overwhelming him. To remain on the defensive would have been bad policy for an army of so great value as the one I then commanded, and I was forced to adopt a course more fruitful in results than the naked one of following him to the Southwest. I had previously submitted to the commander-in-chief a general plan, which amounted substantially to the destruction of Atlanta and the railroad back to Chattanooga, and sallying forth from Atlanta, through the heart of Georgia, to capture one or more of the great Atlantic seaports. This I renewed from Gaylesville, modified somewhat by the change of events.

On the 26th of October, satisfied that Hood had moved westward from Gadsden across Sand Mountain, I detached

the Fourth Corps, Major-General Stanley, and ordered
him to proceed to Chattanooga, and report to Major-General Thomas at Nashville. Subsequently, on the 30th of
October, I also detached the Twenty-third Corps, Major-
General Schofield, with the same destination; and delegated to Major-General Thomas full power over all the troops
subject to my command, except the four corps with which
I designed to move into Georgia. This gave him the two
divisions under A. J. Smith, then in Missouri, but *en route*
for Tennessee; the two corps named, and all the garrisons
in Tennessee, as also all the cavalry of my military division, except one division under Brigadier-General Kilpatrick, which was ordered to rendezvous at Marietta.
Brevet Major-General Wilson had arrived from the Army
of the Potomac, to assume command of the cavalry of my
army, and I dispatched him back to Nashville with all dismounted detachments, and orders as rapidly as possible to
collect the cavalry serving in Kentucky and Tennessee, to
mount, organize, and equip them, and report to Major-
General Thomas for duty. These forces I judged would
enable General Thomas to defend the railroad from Chattanooga back, including Nashville and Decatur, and give
him an army with which he could successfully cope with
Hood, should the latter cross the Tennessee northward.

By the 1st of November, Hood's army had moved from
Gadsden, and made its appearance in the neighborhood of
Decatur, where a feint was made; he then passed on to
Tuscumbia and laid a pontoon bridge opposite Florence. I then began my preparations for the march
through Georgia, having received the sanction of the
commander-in-chief for carrying into effect my plan, the
details of which were explained to all my corps commanders and heads of staff departments, with strict injunctions

of secrecy. I had also communicated full details to General Thomas, and had informed him I would not leave the neighborhood of Kingston until he felt perfectly confident that he was entirely prepared to cope with Hood, should he carry into effect his threatened invasion of Tennessee and Kentucky. I estimated Hood's force at 35,000 infantry and 10,000 cavalry.

I moved the Army of the Tennessee by slow and easy marches on the south of the Coosa, back to the neighborhood of Smyrna camp-ground, and the Fourteenth Corps, General Jeff. C. Davis, to Kingston, whither I repaired in person on the 2d of November. From that point I directed all surplus artillery, all baggage not needed for my contemplated march, all the sick and wounded, refugees, etc., to be sent back to Chattanooga; and the four corps above mentioned, with Kilpatrick's cavalry, were put in the most efficient condition possible for a long and difficult march. This operation consumed the time until the 11th of November, when, every thing being ready, I ordered General Corse, who still remained at Rome, to destroy the bridges there, all foundries, mills, shops, warehouses, or other property that could be useful to an enemy, and to move to Kingston. At the same time the railroad in and about Atlanta, and between the Etowah and the Chattahoochie, was ordered to be utterly destroyed.

The garrisons from Kingston northward were also ordered to draw back to Chattanooga, taking with them all public property and all railroad stock, and to take up the rails from Resaca back, saving them, ready to be replaced whenever future interests should demand. The railroad between the Etowah and the Oostenaula was left untouched, because I thought it more than probable we would find it necessary to reoccupy the country as far forward as the line of the Etowah. Atlanta itself is only of strategic value as long as it is a railroad centre; and as all the railroads leading to it are destroyed, as well as all its foundries, machine-shops, warehouses, depots, etc., it is of no more value than any other point in North Georgia; whereas the line of the Etowah, by reason of its rivers and natural features, possesses an importance which will always continue. From it all parts of Georgia and Alabama can be reached by armies marching with trains down the Coosa or the Chattahoochie valleys.

On the 12th of November my army stood detached and cut off from all communication with the rear. It was composed of four corps, the Fifteenth and Seventeenth, constituting the right wing, under Major General O. O. Howard; the Fourteenth and Twentieth corps, constituting the left wing, under Major-General H. W. Slocum;—of an aggregate strength of 60,000 infantry: one cavalry division, in aggregate strength 5,500, under Brigadier-General Judson Kilpatrick, and the artillery reduced to the minimum of one gun per thousand men.

The whole force moved rapidly and grouped about Atlanta on the 14th November. In the mean time Captain O. M. Poe had thoroughly destroyed Atlanta, save its mere dwelling-houses and churches, and the right wing, with General Kilpatrick's cavalry, was put in motion in the direction of Jonesboro' and McDonough, with orders to make a strong feint on Macon, to cross the Ocmulgee about Planters' Mills, and rendezvous in the neighborhood of Gordon in seven days, exclusive of the day of march. On the same day General Slocum moved with the Twentieth Corps by Decatur and Stone Mountain, with orders to tear up the railroad from Social Circle to Madison, to burn the large and important railroad-bridge across the Oconee, east of Madison, and turn south and reach Milledgeville on the seventh day, exclusive of the day of march.

In person I left Atlanta on the 16th, in company with the Fourteenth Corps, brevet Major-General Jeff. C. Davis, by Lithonia, Covington, and Shady Dale, directly on Milledgeville. All the troops were provided with good wagon-trains, loaded with ammunition, and supplies approximating twenty days' bread, forty days' sugar and coffee, a double allowance of salt for forty days, and beef-cattle equal to forty days' supplies. The wagons were also supplied with about three days' forage in grain. All were instructed, by a judicious system of foraging, to maintain this order of things as long as possible, living chiefly, if not solely, upon the country, which I knew to abound in corn, sweet potatoes, and meats.

My first object was, of course, to place my army in the very heart of Georgia, interposing between Macon and Augusta, and obliging the enemy to divide his forces to defend not only those points, but Millen, Savannah, and Charleston. All my calculations were fully realized. During the 22d General Kilpatrick made a good feint on Macon, driving the enemy within his intrenchments, and then drew back to Griswoldsville, where Walcott's brigade of infantry joined him to cover that flank, while Howard's trains were closing up, and his men scattered, breaking up railroads. The enemy came out of Macon and attacked Walcott in position, but was so roughly handled that he never repeated the experiment. On the eighth day after leaving Atlanta, namely, on the 23d, General Slocum occupied Milledgeville and the important bridge across the Oconee there; and Generals Howard and Kilpatrick were in and about Gordon.

General Howard was then ordered to move eastward,

destroying the railroad thoroughly in his progress as far as Tennille Station, opposite Sandersville, and General Slocum to move to Sandersville by two roads. General Kilpatrick was ordered to Milledgeville, and thence move rapidly eastward, to break the railroad which leads from Millen to Augusta, then to turn upon Millen and rescue our prisoners of war supposed to be confined at that place. I accompanied the Twentieth Corps from Milledgeville to Sandersville, approaching which place, on the 25th, we found the bridges across Buffalo Creek burned, which delayed us three hours. The next day we entered Sandersville, skirmishing with Wheeler's cavalry, which offered little opposition to the advance of the Twentieth and Fourteenth Corps, entering the place almost at the same moment.

General Slocum was then ordered to tear up and destroy the Georgia Central Railroad, from Station No. 13 (Tennille) to Station No. 10, near the crossing of Ogeechee; one of his corps substantially following the railroad, the other by way of Louisville, in support of Kilpatrick's cavalry. In person I shifted to the right wing, and accompanied the Seventeenth Corps, General Blair, on the south of the railroad, till abreast of Station No. 9½ (Barton); General Howard, in person, with the Fifteenth Corps, keeping further to the right, and about one day's march ahead, ready to turn against the flank of any enemy who should oppose our progress.

At Barton I learned that Kilpatrick's cavalry had reached the Augusta Railroad about Waynesborough, where he ascertained that our prisoners had been removed from Millen, and therefore the purpose of rescuing them, upon which we had set our hearts, was an impossibility. But as Wheeler's cavalry had hung around him, and as he had

retired to Louisville to meet our infantry, in pursuance of
my instructions not to risk a battle unless at great advantage, I ordered him to leave his wagons and all encumbrances with the left wing, and moving in the direction of
Augusta, if Wheeler gave him the opportunity, to indulge
him with all the fighting he wanted. General Kilpatrick,
supported by Baird's division of infantry of the Fourteenth
Corps, again moved in the direction of Waynesborough,
and encountering Wheeler in the neighborhood of Thomas's
Station, attacked him in position, driving him from three
successive lines of barricades handsomely through Waynesborough and across Brier Creek, the bridges over which
he burned; and then, with Baird's division, rejoined the
left wing, which in the mean time had been marching by
easy stages of ten miles a day in the direction of Lumpkin's Station and Jacksonboro'.

The Seventeenth Corps took up the destruction of the
railroad at the Ogeechee, near Station No. 10, and continued it to Millen; the enemy offering little or no opposition, although preparation had seemingly been made at
Millen.

On the 3d of December the Seventeenth Corps, which
I accompanied, was at Millen; the Fifteenth Corps, General Howard, was south of the Ogeechee, opposite Station
No. 7 (Scarboro'); the Twentieth Corps, General Slocum,
on the Augusta Railroad, about four miles north of Millen,
near Buckhead Church; and the Fourteenth Corps, General Jeff. C. Davis, in the neighborhood of Lumpkin's
Station, on the Augusta Railroad. All were ordered to
march in the direction of Savannah—the Fifteenth Corps
to continue south of the Ogeechee, the Seventeenth to destroy the railroad as far as Ogeechee Church—and four
days were allowed to reach the line from Ogeechee Church

to the neighborhood of Halley's Ferry, on the Savannah River. All the columns reached their destinations in time, and continued to march on their several roads—General Davis following the Savannah River road, General Slocum the middle road by way of Springfield, General. Blair the railroad, and General Howard still south and west of the Ogeechee, with orders to cross to the east bank opposite "Eden Station," or Station No. 2.

As we approached Savannah the country became more marshy and difficult, and more obstructions were met, in the way of felled trees, where the roads crossed the creek, swamps, or narrow causeways; but our pioneer companies were well organized, and removed the obstructions in an incredibly short time. No opposition from the enemy worth speaking of was encountered until the heads of columns were within fifteen miles of Savannah, where all the roads leading to the city were obstructed more or less by felled timber, with earthworks and artillery. But these were easily turned, and the enemy driven away, so that by the 10th of December the enemy was driven within his lines at Savannah. These followed substantially a swampy creek which empties into the Savannah River about three miles above the city, across to the head of a corresponding stream which empties into the Little Ogeechee. These streams were singularly favorable to the enemy as a cover, being very marshy, and bordered by rice-fields, which were flooded either by the tide-water or by inland ponds, the gates to which were controlled and covered by his heavy artillery.

The only approaches to the city were by five narrow causeways, namely, the two railroads, and the Augusta, the Louisville, and the Ogeechee dirt-roads; all of which were commanded by heavy ordnance, too strong for us to fight with our light field-guns. To assault an enemy of unknown strength at such a disadvantage appeared to me unwise, especially as I had so successfully brought my army, almost unscathed, so great a distance, and could surely attain the same result by the operation of time. I therefore instructed my army commanders to closely invest the city from the north and west, and to reconnoitre well the ground in their fronts, respectively, while I gave my personal attention to opening communications with our fleet, which I knew was waiting for us in Tybee, Wassaw, and Ossabaw sounds.

In approaching Savannah, General Slocum struck the Charleston Railroad near the bridge, and occupied the river-bank as his left flank, where he had captured two of the enemy's river-boats, and had prevented two others (gunboats) from coming down the river to communicate with the city; while General Howard, by his right flank, had broken the Gulf Railroad at Fleming's and way stations, and occupied the railroad itself down to the Little Ogeechee, near " Station No. 1 ;" so that no supplies could reach Savannah by any of its accustomed channels. We, on the contrary, possessed large herds of cattle, which we had brought along or gathered in the country, and our wagons still contained a reasonable amount of breadstuffs and other necessaries, and the fine rice-crops of the Savannah and Ogeechee rivers furnished to our men and animals a large amount of rice and rice-straw. We also held the country to the south and west of the Ogeechee as foraging-ground. Still, communication with the fleet was of vital importance, and I directed General Kilpatrick to cross the Ogeechee by a pontoon bridge, to reconnoitre Fort McAllister, and to proceed to Catherine's Sound, in the direction of Sunbury or Kilkenny Bluff, and open communication with the fleet. General Howard had previously, by my direction, sent one of his best scouts down the Ogeechee in a canoe for a like purpose. But more than this was necessary. We wanted the vessels and their contents; and the Ogeechee River, a navigable stream, close to the rear of our camps, was the proper avenue of supply.

The enemy had burned the road-bridge across the Ogeechee, just below the mouth of the Canoochee, known as "King's Bridge." This was reconstructed in an incredibly short time, in the most substantial manner, by the 58th Indiana, Colonel Buel, under the direction of Captain Reese, of the Engineers Corps, and on the 13th of December the Second division of the Fifteenth Corps, under command of Brigadier-General Hazen, crossed the bridge to the west bank of the Ogeechee, and marched down with orders to carry by assault Fort McAllister, a strong inclosed redoubt, manned by two companies of artillery and three of infantry, in all about two hundred men, and mounting twenty-three guns *en barbette*, and one mortar. General Hazen reached the vicinity of Fort McAllister about 1 P.M., deployed his division about that place, with both flanks resting upon the river; posted his skirmishers judiciously behind the trunks of trees whose branches had been used for *abattis*, and about 5 P.M. assaulted the place with nine regiments at three points; all of them successfully. I witnessed the assault from a rice-mill on the opposite bank of the river, and can bear testimony to the handsome manner in which it was accomplished.

Up to this time we had not communicated with our fleet. From the signal-station at the rice-mill our officers had looked for two days over the rice-fields and salt marsh in the direction of Ossabaw Sound, but could see nothing of it. But while watching the preparations for the assault on Fort McAllister, we discovered in the distance what seemed to be the smoke-stack of a steamer, which became more and more distinct. Until about the very moment of the assault she was plainly visible below the fort, and our signal was answered. As soon as I saw our colors fairly planted upon the walls of Fort McAllister, in company with General Howard, I went in a small boat down to the fort and met General Hazen, who had not yet communicated with the gunboat below, as it was shut out to him by a point of timber. Determined to communicate that night, I got another small boat and a crew, and pulled down the river till I found the tug Dandelion, Captain Williamson, U. S. N., who informed me that Captain Duncan, who had been sent by General Howard, had succeeded in reaching Admiral Dahlgren and General Foster, and that he was expecting them hourly in Ossabaw Sound. After making communications to those officers, and a short communication to the War Department, I returned to Fort McAllister that night, and before daylight was overtaken by Major Strong, of General Foster's staff, advising me that General Foster had arrived in the Ogeechee, near Fort McAllister, and was very anxious to meet me on board his boat. I accordingly returned with him, and met General Foster on board the steamer Nemaha; and, after consultation, determined to proceed with him down the Sound, in hopes to meet Admiral Dahlgren. But we did not meet him until we reached Wassaw Sound, about noon. I there went on board the admiral's flagship, the Harvest Moon, after having arranged with General Foster to send us from Hilton Head some siege ordnance and some boats suitable for navigating the Ogeechee River. Admiral Dahlgren very kindly furnished me with all the data concerning his fleet and the numerous forts that guarded the inland channels between the sea and Savannah. I explained to him how completely Savannah was invested at all points, save only the plank-road on the South Carolina shore, known as the "Union Causeway," which I thought I could reach from my left flank across the Savannah River. I explained to him that if he would simply engage the attention of the forts along Wilmington Channel, at Beaulieu and Rosedew, I thought I could carry the defences of Savannah by assault as soon as the heavy ordnance arrived from Hilton Head. On the 15th the admiral carried me back to Fort McAllister, whence I returned to our lines in the rear of Savannah.

Having received and carefully considered all the reports of division commanders, I determined to assault the lines of the enemy as soon as my heavy ordnance came from Port Royal, first making a formal demand for surrender. On the 17th, a number of thirty-pounder Parrott guns having reached King's Bridge, I proceeded in person to the headquarters of Major-General Slocum, on the Augusta Road, and dispatched thence into Savannah, by flag of truce, a formal demand for the surrender of the place, and on the following day received an answer from General Hardee refusing to surrender.

In the mean time further reconnoissances from our left flank had demonstrated that it was impracticable or unwise to push any considerable force across the Savannah River, for the enemy held the river opposite the city with ironclad gunboats, and could destroy any pontoons laid down by us between Hutchinson's Island and the South Carolina shore, which would isolate any force sent over from that flank. I therefore ordered General Slocum to get into position the siege-guns, and make all the preparations necessary to assault, and report to me the earliest moment when he could be ready; while I should proceed rapidly round by the right and make arrangements to occupy the Union Causeway from the direction of Port Royal. General Foster had already established a division of troops on the peninsula or neck between the Coosawatchie and Tullifinney rivers, at the head of Broad River, from which position he could reach the railroad with his artillery.

I went to Port Royal in person, and made arrangements to re-enforce that command by one or more divisions, under a proper officer; to assault and carry the railroad, and thence turn towards Savannah, until it occupied the causeway in question. I went on board the admiral's flagship, the Harvest Moon, which put out to sea the night of the 20th. But the wind was high, and increased during the night, so that the pilot judged Ossabaw Bar impassable, and ran into the Tybee, whence we proceeded through the inland channels into Wassaw Sound, and thence through Romney Marsh. But the ebb-tide caught the Harvest Moon, and she was unable to make the passage. Admiral Dahlgren took me in his barge, and pulling in the direction of Vernon River, we met the army-tug Red Legs, bearing a message from my adjutant, Captain Dayton, of that morning, the 21st, to the effect that our troops were in possession of the enemy's lines, and were advancing without opposition into Savannah, the enemy having evacuated the place during the previous night.

Admiral Dahlgren proceeded up the Vernon River in his barge, while I transferred to the tug, in which I proceeded to Fort McAllister, and thence to the rice-mill; and on the morning of the 22d rode into the city of Savannah, already occupied by our troops.

I was very much disappointed that Hardee had escaped with his garrison, and had to content myself with the material fruits of victory without the cost of life which would have attended a general assault. The substantial results will be more clearly set forth in the tabular statements of heavy ordinance and other public property acquired, and it will suffice here to state that the important city of Savannah, with its valuable harbor and river, was the chief object of the campaign. With it we acquire all the forts and heavy ordinance in its vicinity, with large stores of ammunition, shot and shells, cotton, rice, and other valuable products of the country. We also gain locomotives and cars, which, though of little use to us in the present condition of the railroads, are a serious loss to the enemy: as well as four steamboats gained, and the loss to the enemy of the iron-clad Savannah, one ram, and three transports, blown up or burned by them the night before.

Formal demand having been made for the surrender, and having been refused, I contend that every thing within the line of intrenchments belongs to the United States; and I shall not hesitate to use it, if necessary, for public purposes. But inasmuch as the inhabitants generally have manifested a friendly disposition, I shall disturb them as little as possible consistently with the military rights of present and future military commanders, without remitting in the least our just rights as captors.

After having made the necessary orders for the disposition of the troops in and about Savannah, I ordered Captain O. M. Poe, chief engineer, to make a thorough examination of the enemy's works in and about Savannah, with a view to making it conform to our future uses. New lines of defences will be built, embracing the city proper, Forts Jackson, Thunderbolt, and Pulaski retained, with slight modifications in their armament and

4*

rear defences. All the rest of the enemy's forts will be dismantled and destroyed, and their heavy ordinance transferred to Hilton Head, where it can be more easily guarded. Our base of supplies will be established in Savannah, as soon as the very difficult obstructions placed in the river can be partially removed. These obstructions at present offer a very serious impediment to the commerce of Savannah, consisting of crib-work of logs and timber heavily bolted together, and filled with the cobble-stones which formerly paved the streets of Savannah. All the channels below the city were found more or less filled with torpedoes, which have been removed by order of Admiral Dahlgren, so that Savannah already fulfils the important part it was designed in our plans for the future.

In thus sketching the course of events connected with this campaign, I have purposely passed lightly over the march from Atlanta to the sea-shore, because it was made in four or more columns, sometimes at a distance of fifteen or twenty miles from each other, and it was impossible for me to attend but one. Therefore I have left it to the army and corps commanders to describe in their own language the events which attended the march of their respective columns. These reports are herewith submitted, and I beg to refer to them for further details. I would merely sum up the advantages which I conceive have accrued to us by this march.

Our former labors in North Georgia had demonstrated the truth that no large army, carrying with it the necessary stores and baggage, can overtake and capture an inferior force of the enemy in his own country. Therefore no alternative was left me but the one I adopted, namely, to divide my forces, and with one part act offensively against the enemy's resources, while with the other I should act defensively, and invite the enemy to attack, risking the chances of battle. In this conclusion I have been singularly sustained by the .results. General Hood, who, as I have heretofore described, had moved to the westward near Tuscumbia, with a view to decoy me away from Georgia, finding himself mistaken, was forced to choose, either to pursue me or to act offensively against the other part left in Tennessee. He adopted the latter course ; and General Thomas has wisely and well fulfilled his part in the grand scheme in drawing Hood well up into Tennessee until he could concentrate all his own troops and then turn upon Hood, as he has done, and destroy or fatally cripple his army. That part of my army is so far removed from me, that I leave, with perfect confidence, its management and history to General Thomas.

I was thereby left with a well-appointed army to sever the enemy's only remaining railroad communications eastward and westward, for over 100 miles—namely, the Georgia State Railroad, which is broken up from Fairburn Station to Madison and the Oconee, and the Central Railroad from Gordon clear to Savannah, with numerous breaks on the latter road from Gordon to Eatonton, and from Millen to Augusta, and the Savannah and Gulf Railroad. We have also consumed the corn and fodder in the region of country thirty miles on either side of a line from Atlanta to Savannah ; as also the sweet potatoes, cattle, hogs, sheep, and poultry, and have carried away more than 10,000 horses and mules, as well as a countless number of their slaves. I estimate the damage done to the State of Georgia and its military resources at $100,000,000, at least $20,000,000 of which has inured to our advantage, and the remainder is simple waste and destruction. This may seem a hard species of warfare, but it brings the sad realities of war home to those who have been directly or indirectly instrumental in involving us in its attendant calamities.

This campaign has also placed this branch of my army in a position from which other great military results may be attempted, besides leaving in Tennessee and North Alabama a force which is amply sufficient to meet all the chances of war in that region of our country.

Since the capture of Atlanta my staff is unchanged, save that General Barry, chief of artillery, has been absent sick since our leaving Kingston. Surgeon Moore, United States Army, is chief medical director, in place of Surgeon Kittoe, relieved to resume his proper duties as a medical inspector. Major Hitchcock, A. A. G., has also been added to my staff, and has been of great assistance in the field and office. Captain Dayton still remains as my adjutant-general. All have, as formerly, fulfilled their parts to my entire satisfaction.

In the body of my army I feel a just pride. Generals Howard and Slocum are gentlemen of singular capacity and intelligence, thorough soldiers and patriots, working day and night, not for themselves, but for their country and their men. General Kilpatrick, who commanded the cavalry of this army, has handled it with spirit and dash, to my entire satisfaction, and kept a superior force of the enemy's cavalry from even approaching our infantry columns or wagon-trains. His report is full and graphic. All the division and brigade commanders merit my personal and official thanks, and I shall spare no efforts to secure them commissions equal to the rank they have exercised so well. As to the rank and file, they seem so full of confidence in themselves that I doubt if they want a compliment from me; but I must do them the justice to say that, whether called on to fight, to march, to wade streams, to make roads, clear out obstructions, build bridges, make " corduroy," or tear up railroads, they have done it with alacrity and a degree of cheerfulness unsurpassed. A little loose in foraging, they " did some things they ought not to have done," yet on the whole they have supplied the wants of the army with as little violence as could be expected, and as little loss as I calculated. Some of these foraging-parties had encounters with the enemy which would, in ordinary times, rank as respectable battles. The behavior of our troops in Savannah has been so manly, so quiet, so perfect, that I take it as the best evidence of discipline and true courage. Never was a hostile city, filled with women and children, occupied by a large army with less disorder, or more system, order, and good government. The same general and generous spirit of confidence and good feeling pervades the army which it has ever afforded me special pleasure to report on former occasions.

I avail myself of this occasion to express my heartfelt thanks to Admiral Dahlgren and the officers and men of his fleet, as also to General Foster and his command, for the hearty welcome given us on our arrival at the coast, and for their steady and prompt co-operation in all measures tending to the result accomplished.

I send herewith a map of the country through which we have passed; reports from General Howard, General Slocum, and General Kilpatrick, and their subordinates respectively; with the usual lists of captured property, killed, wounded, and missing, prisoners of war taken and rescued; as also copies of all papers illustrating the campaign. All of which are respectfully submitted by

Your obedient servant,

W. T. SHERMAN, Major-General.

III.

FROM SAVANNAH TO GOLDSBORO',

THROUGH THE CAROLINAS.

HEADQUARTERS MIL. DIV. OF THE MISSISSIPPI,
Goldsboro', N. C., April 4, 1865.

GENERAL—I must now endeavor to group the events of the past three months connected with the armies under my command, in order that you may have as clear an understanding of the late campaign as the case admits of. The reports of the subordinate commanders will enable you to fill up the picture.

I have heretofore explained how, in the progress of our arms, I was enabled to leave in the West an army under Major-General George H. Thomas of sufficient strength to meet emergencies in that quarter, while in person I conducted another army, composed of the Fourteenth, Fifteenth, Seventeenth, and Twentieth corps, and Kilpatrick's division of cavalry, to the Atlantic slope, aiming to approach the grand theatre of war in Virginia by the time the season would admit of military operations in that latitude. The first lodgment on the coast was made at Savannah, strongly fortified and armed, and valuable to us as a good seaport, with its navigable stream inland. Near a month was consumed there in refitting the army, and in making the proper disposition of captured property, and other local matters; but by the 15th of January I was all ready to resume the march. Preliminary to this, General

Howard, commanding the right wing, was ordered to em-
bark his command at Thunderbolt, transport it to Beaufort,
South Carolina, and thence, by the 15th of January, make
a lodgment on the Charleston Railroad, at or near Pocotaligo. This was accomplished punctually, at little cost, by
the Seventeenth Corps, Major-General Blair, and a depot
for supplies was established near the mouth of Pocotaligo
Creek, with easy water communication back to Hilton Head.

The left wing, Major-General Slocum, and the cavalry,
Major-General Kilpatrick, were ordered to rendezvous
about the same time near Robertsville and Coosawhatchie,
South Carolina, with a depot of supplies at Pureysburg or
Sister's Ferry, on the Savannah River. General Slocum
had a good pontoon bridge constructed opposite the city,
and the " Union Causeway," leading through the low rice-
fields opposite Savannah, was repaired and " corduroyed."
But before the time appointed to start, the heavy rains of
January had swelled the river, broken the pontoon bridge,
and overflowed the whole " bottom," so that the causeway
was four feet under water, and General Slocum was compelled to look higher up for a passage over the Savannah
River. He moved up to Sister's Ferry, but even there the
river, with its overflowed bottoms, was near three miles
wide, and he did not succeed in getting his whole wing
across until during the first week of February.

In the mean time, General Grant had sent me Grover's
division of the Nineteenth Corps to garrison Savannah, and
had drawn the Twenty-third Corps, Major-General Schofield,
from Tennessee, and sent it to re-enforce the commands of
Major-Generals Terry and Palmer, operating on the coast
of North Carolina, to prepare the way for my coming.

On the 18th of January I transferred the forts and city
of Savannah to Major-General Foster, commanding the

Department of the South, imparted to him my plans of
operation, and instructed him how to follow my movements
inland, by occupying in succession the city of Charleston
and such other points along the seacoast as would be of
any military value to us. The combined naval and land
forces under Admiral Porter and General Terry had, on
the 15th of January, captured Fort Fisher and the rebel
forts at the mouth of Cape Fear River, giving me an additional point of security on the seacoast. But I had
already resolved in my own mind, and had so advised General Grant, that I would undertake at one stride to make
Goldsboro', and open communication with the sea by the
Newbern Railroad, and had ordered Colonel W. W.
Wright, superintendent of military railroads, to proceed
in advance to Newbern, and to be prepared to extend the
railroad out from Newbern to Goldsboro' by the 15th of
March. On the 19th of January all preparations were
complete, and the orders of march given. My chief
quartermaster and commissary, Generals Easton and Beckwith, were ordered to complete the supplies at Sister's
Ferry and Pocotaligo, and then to follow our movement
coastwise, looking for my arrival at Goldsboro', North
Carolina, about March 15, and opening communication
with me from Morehead City.

On the 22d of January I embarked at Savannah for
Hilton Head, where I held a conference with Admiral
Dahlgren, United States Navy, and Major-General Foster,
commanding the Department of the South, and next day
proceeded to Beaufort, riding out thence on the 24th to
Pocotaligo, where the Seventeenth Corps, Major-General
Blair, was encamped. The Fifteenth Corps was somewhat
scattered—Woods' and Hazen's divisions at Beaufort, John
E. Smith marching from Savannah by the coast road, and

Corse still at Savannah, cut off by the storms and freshet in the river. ·On the 25th a demonstration was made against the Combahee Ferry and railroad-bridge across the Salkehatchie, merely to amuse the enemy, who had evidently adopted that river as his defensive line against our supposed *objective*, the city of Charleston. I reconnoitred the line in person, and saw that the heavy rains had swollen the river so that water stood in the swamps, for a breadth of more than a mile, at a depth of from one to twenty feet. Not having the remotest intention of approaching Charleston, a comparatively small force was able, by seeming preparations to cross over, to keep in their front a considerable force of the enemy disposed to contest our advance on Charleston. On the 27th I rode to the camp of General Hatch's division of Foster's command, on the Tullafulney and Coosawhatchie rivers, and directed those places to be evacuated, as no longer of any use to us. That division was then moved to Pocotaligo to keep up the feints already begun, until we should with the right wing move higher up and cross the Salkehatchie about Rivers' or Broxton's bridge. On the 29th I learned that the roads back of Savannah had at last become sufficiently free of the flood to admit of General Slocum putting his wing in motion, and that he was already approaching Sister's Ferry, whither a gunboat, the Pontiac, Captain Luce, kindly furnished by Admiral Dahlgren, had preceded him to cover the crossing. In the mean time, three divisions of the Fifteenth Corps had closed up at Pocotaligo, and the right wing had loaded its wagons and was ready to start. I therefore directed General Howard to move one corps, the Seventeenth, along the Salkehatchie, as high up as Rivers' Bridge, and the other, the Fifteenth, by Hickory Hill, Loper's Cross-roads, Anglesey Post-office, and Beaufort's Bridge. Hatch's division was ordered to remain at Pocotaligo, feigning at the Salkehatchie railroad-bridge and ferry, until our movement turned the enemy's position and forced him to fall behind the Edisto.

The Seventeenth and Fifteenth corps drew out of camp on the 31st of January, but the real march began on the 1st of February. All the roads northward had for weeks been held by Wheeler's cavalry, who had by details of negro laborers felled trees, burned bridges, and made obstructions to impede our march. But so well organized were our pioneer battalions, and so strong and intelligent our men, that obstructions seemed only to quicken their progress. Felled trees were removed and bridges rebuilt by the heads of columns before the rear could close up. On the 2d of February the Fifteenth Corps reached Loper's Cross-roads, and the Seventeenth was at Rivers' Bridge. From Loper's Cross-roads I communicated with General Slocum, still struggling with the floods of the Savannah River at Sister's Ferry. He had two divisions of the Twentieth Corps, General Williams, on the east bank, and was enabled to cross over on his pontoons the cavalry of Kilpatrick. General Williams was ordered to Beaufort's Bridge, by way of Lawtonville and Allendale, Kilpatrick to Blackville *via* Barnwell, and General Slocum to hurry the crossing at Sister's Ferry as much as possible, and overtake the right wing on the South Carolina Railroad. General Howard, with the right wing, was directed to cross the Salkehatchie and push rapidly for the South Carolina Railroad, at or near Midway. The enemy held the line of the Salkehatchie in force, having infantry and artillery intrenched at Rivers' and Beaufort's bridges. The Seventeenth Corps was ordered to carry Rivers' Bridge, and the Fifteenth Corps Beaufort's Bridge. The former position was carried promptly and skilfully by Mower's and Giles A. Smith's divisions of the Seventeenth Corps, on the 3d of February, by crossing the swamp, nearly three miles wide, with water varying from knee to shoulder deep. The weather was bitter cold, and Generals Mower and Smith led their divisions in person, on foot, waded the swamp, made a lodgment below the bridge, and turned on the rebel brigade which guarded it, driving it in confusion and disorder towards Branchville. Our casualties were one officer and seventeen men killed, and seventy men wounded, who were sent to Pocotaligo. The line of the Salkehatchie being thus broken, the enemy retreated at once behind the Edisto, at Branchville, and the whole army was pushed rapidly to the South Carolina Railroad at Midway, Bamberg (or Lowry's Station), and Graham's Station. The Seventeenth Corps, by threatening Branchville, forced the enemy to burn the railroad bridge, and Walker's Bridge below, across the Edisto. All hands were at once set to work to destroy railroad track. From the 7th to the 10th of February this work was thoroughly prosecuted by the Seventeenth Corps from the Edisto up to Bamberg, and by the Fifteenth Corps from Bamberg up to Blackville. In the mean time General Kilpatrick had brought his cavalry rapidly by Barnwell to Blackville, and had turned towards Aiken, with orders to threaten Augusta, but not to be drawn needlessly into a serious battle. This he skilfully accomplished, skirmishing heavily with Wheeler's cavalry, first at Blackville, and afterwards at Williston and Aiken. General Williams, with two divisions of the Twentieth Corps, marched to the South Carolina Railroad at Graham's Station, on the 8th, and General Slocum reached Blackville on the 10th. The destruction of the railroad was continued by the left wing from

Blackville up to Windsor. By the 11th of February all the army was on the railroad from Midway to Johnson's Station, thereby dividing the enemy's forces, which still remained at Branchville and Charleston on the one hand, Aiken and Augusta on the other.

We then began the movement on Orangeburg. The Seventeeth Corps crossed the South Fork of Edisto River at Binnaker's Bridge, and moved straight for Orangeburg, while the Fifteenth Corps crossed at Holman's Bridge and moved to Poplar Springs in support. The left wing and cavalry were still at work on the railroad, with orders to cross the South Edisto at New and Guignard's bridges, move to the Orangeburg and Edgefield Road, and there await the result of the attack on Orangeburg. On the 12th the Seventeenth Corps found the enemy intrenched in front of the Orangeburg Bridge, but swept him away by a dash, and followed him, forcing him across the bridge, which was partially burned. Behind the bridge was a battery in position, covered by a cotton and earth parapet, with wings as far as could be seen. General Blair held one division (Giles A. Smith's) close up to the Edisto, and moved the other two to a point about two miles below, where he crossed Force's division by a pontoon bridge, holding Mower's in support. As soon as Force emerged from the swamp, the enemy gave ground, and Giles Smith's division gained the bridge, crossed over, and occupied the enemy's parapet. He soon repaired the bridge, and by 4 P.M. the whole corps was in Orangeburg, and had begun the work of destruction on the railroad. Blair was ordered to destroy this railroad effectually up to Lewisville, and to push the enemy across the Congaree, and force him to burn the bridges, which he did on the 14th; and without wasting time or labor on Branchville or

Charleston, which I knew the enemy could no longer hold, I turned all the columns straight on Columbia. The Seventeenth Corps followed the State road, and the Fifteenth crossed the North Edisto from Poplar Springs at Schilling's Bridge, above the mouth of "Cawcaw Swamp" Creek, and took a country road which came into the State Road at Zeigler's. On the 15th, the Fifteenth Corps found the enemy in a strong position at Little Congaree bridge (across Congaree Creek), with a *tête-de-pont* on the south side, and a well-constructed fort on the north side, commanding the bridge with artillery. The ground in front was very bad, level, and clear, with a fresh deposit of mud from a recent overflow. General Charles R. Woods, who commanded the leading division, succeeded, however, in turning the flank of the *tête-de-pont*, by sending Stone's brigade through a cypress swamp to the left; and following up the retreating enemy promptly, he got possession of the bridge and the fort beyond. The bridge had been partially damaged by fire, and had to be repaired for the passage of artillery, so that night closed in before the head of the column reached the bridge across Congaree River in front of Columbia. That night the enemy shelled our camps from a battery on the east side of the Congaree above Granby. Early next morning (February 16) the head of the column reached the bank of the Congaree, opposite Columbia, but too late to save the fine bridge which spanned the river at that point. It was burned by the enemy. While waiting for the pontoons to come to the front we could see people running about the streets of Columbia, and occasionally small bodies of cavalry, but no masses. A single gun of Captain De Grass's battery was firing at their cavalry squads, but I checked his firing, limiting him to a few shots at the unfinished State-House walls, and a few shells at the railroad depot to scatter the people who were seen carrying away sacks of corn and meal that we needed. There was no white flag or manifestations of surrender. I directed General Howard not to cross directly in front of Columbia, but to cross the Saluda at the Factory, three miles above, and afterwards Broad River, so as to approach Columbia from the north. Within an hour of the arrival of General Howard's head of column at the river opposite Columbia, the head of column of the left wing also appeared, and I directed General Slocum to cross the Saluda at Zion Church, and thence to take roads direct for Winnsboro', breaking up *en route* the railroad and bridges about Alston.

General Howard effected a crossing of the Saluda, near the Factory, on the 16th, skirmishing with cavalry, and the same night made a flying bridge across Broad River, about three miles above Columbia, by which he crossed over Stone's brigade, of Wood's division, Fifteenth Corps. Under cover of this brigade a pontoon bridge was laid on the morning of the 17th. I was in person at this bridge, and at 11 A.M., learned that the mayor of Columbia had come out in a carriage, and made a formal surrender of the city to Colonel Stone, 25th Iowa infantry, commanding Third brigade, First division, Fifteenth Corps. About the same time a small party of the Seventeenth Corps had crossed the Congaree in a skiff, and entered Columbia from a point immediately west. In anticipation of the occupation of the city, I had made written orders to General Howard touching the conduct of the troops. These were to destroy absolutely all arsenals and public property not needed for our own use, as well as all railroads, depots, and machinery useful in war to an enemy, but to spare all dwellings, colleges, schools, asylums, and harmless private property. I was the first to cross the pontoon bridge, and in company with General Howard rode into the city. The day was clear, but a perfect tempest of wind was raging. The brigade of Colonel Stone was already in the city, and was properly posted. Citizens and soldiers were on the streets, and general good order prevailed. General Wade Hampton, who commanded the Confederate rear-guard of cavalry, had, in anticipation of our capture of Columbia, ordered that all cotton, public and private, should be moved into the streets and fired, to prevent our making use of it. Bales were piled everywhere, the rope and bagging cut, and tufts of cotton were blown about in the wind, lodging in the trees and against houses, so as to resemble a snow-storm. Some of these piles of cotton were burning, especially one in the very heart of the city, near the Courthouse, but the fire was partially subdued by the labor of our soldiers. During the day the Fifteenth Corps passed through Columbia and out on the Camden road. The Seventeenth did not enter the town at all; and, as I have before stated, the left wing and cavalry did not come within two miles of the town.

Before one single public building had been fired by order, the smoldering fires, set by Hampton's order, were rekindled by the wind, and communicated to the buildings around. About dark they began to spread, and got beyond the control of the brigade on duty within the city. The whole of Woods' division was brought in, but it was found impossible to check the flames, which, by midnight, had become unmanageable, and raged until about 4 A. M., when the wind subsiding, they were got under control. I was up nearly all night, and saw Generals Howard, Logan, Woods, and others, laboring to save houses and protect families thus suddenly deprived of shelter, and of bedding and wearing apparel. I disclaim on the part of my army any agency in this fire, but on the contrary claim that we saved what of Columbia remains unconsumed. And without hesitation I charge General Wade Hampton with having burned his own city of Columbia, not with a malicious intent, or as the manifestation of a silly "Roman stoicism," but from folly and want of sense in filling it with lint, cotton, and tinder. Our officers and men on duty worked well to extinguish the flames; but others not on duty, including the officers who had long been imprisoned there, rescued by us, may have assisted in spreading the fire after it had once begun, and may have indulged in unconcealed joy to see the ruin of the capital of South Carolina. During the 18th and 19th, the arsenal, railroad depots, machine shops, foundries, and other buildings were properly destroyed by detailed working parties, and the railroad track torn up and destroyed down to Kingsville and the Wateree Bridge, and up in the direction of Winnsboro'.

At the same time the left wing and cavalry had crossed the Saluda and Broad rivers, breaking up railroad about Alston, and as high up as the bridge across Broad River on the Spartanburg road, the main body moving straight for Winnsboro', which General Slocum reached on the 21st of February. He caused the railroad to be destroyed up to Blackstakes Depot, and then turned to Rocky Mount, on the Catawba River. The Twentieth Corps reached Rocky Mount on the 22d, laid a pontoon bridge, and crossed over during the 23d. Kilpatrick's cavalry followed, and crossed over in a terrible rain during the night of the 23d, and moved up to Lancaster, with orders to keep up the delusion of a general movement on Charlotte, North Carolina, to which General Beauregard and all the cavalry of the enemy had retreated from Columbia. I was also aware that Cheatham's corps, of Hood's old army, was aiming to make a junction with Beauregard at Charlotte, having been cut off by our rapid movement on Columbia and Winnsboro'. From the 23d to the 26th we had heavy rains, swelling the rivers and making the roads almost impassable. The Twentieth Corps reached Hanging Rock on the 26th, and waited there for the Fourteenth Corps to get across the Catawba. The heavy rains had so swollen the river that the pontoon bridge broke, and General Davis had very hard work to restore it and get his command across. At last he succeeded, and the left wing was all put in motion for Cheraw. In the mean time the right wing had broken up the railroad to Winnsboro', and thence turned for Peay's Ferry, where it was crossed over the Catawba before the heavy rains set in, the Seventeenth Corps moving straight on Cheraw *via* Young's bridge, and the Fifteenth Corps by Tiller's and Kelly's bridges. From this latter corps detachments were sent into Camden to burn the bridge over the Wateree, with the railroad depot, stores, &c. A small force of mounted men under Captain Duncan was also dispatched to make a dash and interrupt the railroad from Charleston to Florence, but it met Butler's division of cavalry, and after a sharp night-skirmish on Mount Elon was compelled to return unsuccessful. Much bad road was encountered at Lynch's Creek, which delayed the right wing about the same length of time as the left wing had been at the Catawba. On the 2d of March the leading division of the Twentieth Corps entered Chesterfield, skirmishing with Butler's division of cavalry, and the next day about noon the Seventeenth Corps entered Cheraw, the enemy retreating across the Pedee and burning the bridge at that point. At Cheraw we found much ammunition and many guns, which had

5

been brought from Charleston on the evacuation of that
city. These were destroyed, as also the railroad trestles and
bridges down as far as Darlington. An expedition of mounted infantry was also sent down to Florence, but it encountered both cavalry and infantry, and returned having only
broken up in part the branch road from Florence to Cheraw.

Without unnecessary delay the columns were again put
in motion, directed on Fayetteville, North Carolina, the
right wing crossing the Pedee at Cheraw and the left wing
and cavalry at Sneedsboro'. General Kilpatrick was
ordered to keep well on the left flank, and the Fourteenth
Corps, moving by Love's Bridge, was given the right to
enter and occupy Fayetteville first. The weather continued
unfavorable and roads bad, but the Fourteenth and Seventeenth Corps reached Fayetteville on the 11th of March,
skirmishing with Wade Hampton's cavalry, that covered
the rear of Hardee's retreating army, which as usual had
crossed Cape Fear River, burning the bridge. During the
march from Pedee, General Kilpatrick had kept his cavalry
well on the left and exposed flank. During the night of
the 9th of March his three brigades were divided to picket
the roads. General Hampton detecting this, rushed in at
daylight and gained possession of the camp of Colonel
Spencer's brigade, and the house in which General Kilpatrick and Colonel Spencer had their quarters. The surprise
was complete, but General Kilpatrick quickly succeeded in
rallying his men, on foot, in a swamp near by, and by a
prompt attack, well followed up, regained his artillery,
horses, camp, and every thing save some prisoners whom
the enemy carried off, leaving their dead on the ground.

The 12th, 13th, and 14th were passed at Fayetteville,
destroying absolutely the United States arsenal and the
vast amount of machinery which had formerly belonged to

the Harper's Ferry United States arsenal. Every building was knocked down and burned, and every piece of machinery utterly broken up and ruined by the First Regiment Michigan Engineers, under the immediate supervision of Colonel O. M. Poe, chief engineer. Much valuable property of great use to the enemy was here destroyed or cast into the river.

Up to this period I had perfectly succeeded in interposing my superior army between the scattered parts of the enemy. But I was then aware that the fragments that had left Columbia under Beauregard had been reinforced by Cheatham's corps from the West, and the garrison of Augusta, and that ample time had been given to move them to my front and flank about Raleigh. Hardee had also succeeded in getting across Cape Fear River ahead of me, and could therefore complete the junction with the other armies of Johnston and Hoke in North Carolina. And the whole, under the command of the skilful and experienced Joe Johnston, made up an army superior to me in cavalry, and formidable enough in artillery and infantry to justify me in extreme caution in making the last step necessary to complete the march I had undertaken.

Previous to reaching Fayetteville I had dispatched to Wilmington from Laurel Hill Church two of our best scouts with intelligence of our position and my general plans. Both of these messengers reached Wilmington, and on the morning of the 12th of March the army-tug Davidson, Captain Ainsworth, reached Fayetteville from Wilmington, bringing me full intelligence of events from the outer world. On the same day this tug carried back to General Terry, at Wilmington, and General Schofield, at Newbern, my dispatches to the effect that on Wednesday, the 15th, we would move for Goldsboro', *feigning* on

Raleigh, and ordering them to march straight for Golds-boro', which I expected to reach about the 20th. The same day the gunboat Eolus, Captain Young, United States navy, also reached Fayetteville, and through her I continued to have communication with Wilmington until the day of our actual departure. While the work of destruction was going on at Fayetteville two pontoon bridges were laid across Cape Fear River, one opposite the town, the other three miles below.

General Kilpatrick was ordered to move up the plank-road to and beyond Averasboro'. He was to be followed by four divisions of the left wing, with as few wagons as possible ; the rest of the train, under escort of the two remaining divisions of that wing, to take a shorter and more direct road to Goldsboro'. In like manner General Howard was ordered to send his trains, under good escort, well to the right, towards Faison's Depot and Goldsboro', and to hold four divisions *light*, ready to go to the aid of the left wing if attacked while in motion. The weather continued very bad, and the roads had become mere quagmire. Almost every foot of it had to be corduroyed to admit the passage of wheels. Still, time was so important that punctually, according to order, the columns moved out from Cape Fear River on Wednesday, the 15th of March. I accompanied General Slocum, who, preceded by Kilpatrick's cavalry, moved up the river or plank-road that day to Kyle's Landing, Kilpatrick skirmishing heavily with the enemy's rear-guard about three miles beyond, near Taylor's Hole Creek. At General Kilpatrick's request, General Slocum sent forward a brigade of infantry to hold a line of barricades.

Next morning the column advanced in the same order, and developed the enemy, with artillery, infantry, and cavalry, in an intrenched position in front of the point where the road branches off towards Goldsboro' through Bentonville. On an inspection of the map it was manifest that Hardee in retreating from Fayetteville had halted in the narrow swampy neck between Cape Fear and South rivers in the hopes to hold me, to save time for the concentration of Johnston's armies at some point to his rear—namely, Raleigh, Smithfield, or Goldsboro'. Hardee's force was estimated at twenty thousand men. It was necessary to dislodge him that we might have the use of the Goldsboro' road, as also to keep up the feint on Raleigh as long as possible. General Slocum was therefore ordered to press and carry the position, only difficult by reason of the nature of the ground, which was so soft that horses would sink everywhere, and even men could hardly make their way over the common pine-barren.

The Twentieth Corps, General Williams, had the lead, and Ward's division the advance. This was deployed, and the skirmish line developed the position of a brigade of Charleston heavy artillery, armed as infantry (Rhett's), posted across the road behind a light parapet, with a battery of guns enfilading the approach across a cleared field. General Williams sent a brigade (Case's) by a circuit to his left that turned this line, and, by a quick charge, broke the brigade, which rapidly retreated back to a second line better built and more strongly held. A battery of artillery (Winninger's) well-posted, under the immediate direction of Major Reynolds, chief of artillery of the Twentieth Corps, did good execution on the retreating brigade; and, on advancing Ward's division over this ground, General Williams captured three guns and two hundred and seventeen prisoners, of which sixty-eight were wounded, and left in a house near by with a rebel officer, four men, and five days' rations. One hundred and eight rebel dead were buried by us. As Ward's division advanced, he developed a second and a stronger line, when Jackson's division was deployed forward on the right of Ward, and the two divisions of Jeff. C. Davis's (Fourteenth) corps on the left, well towards the Cape Fear. At the same time Kilpatrick, who was acting in concert with General Williams, was ordered to draw back his cavalry and mass it on the extreme right, and in concert with Jackson's right, to feel forward for the Goldsboro' road. He got a brigade on the road, but it was attacked by McLaws' rebel division furiously, and though it fought well and hard, the brigade drew back to the flank of the infantry. The whole line advanced late in the afternoon, drove the enemy well within his intrenched line, and pressed him so hard, that next morning he was gone, having retreated in a miserable stormy night over the worst of roads. Ward's division of infantry followed to and through Averasboro', developing the fact that Hardee had retreated, not on Raleigh, but on Smithfield. I had the night before directed Kilpatrick to cross South River at a mill-dam to our right and rear, and move up on the east side towards Elevation. General Slocum reports his aggregate loss in the affair known as that of Averasboro', at twelve officers and sixty-five men killed, and four hundred and seventy-seven wounded. We lost no prisoners. The enemy's loss can be inferred from his dead (one hundred and eight) left for us to bury. Leaving Ward's division to keep up a show of pursuit, Slocum's column was turned to the right, built a bridge across the swollen South River, and took the Goldsboro' road, Kilpatrick crossing to the north, in the direction of Elevation, with orders to move eastward, watching that flank. In the mean time the wagon-trains and guards, as also Howard's column, were

wallowing along the miry roads towards Bentonville and
Goldsboro'. The enemy's infantry, as before stated, had
retreated across our front in the same direction, burning
the bridges across Mill Creek. I continued with the head
of Slocum's column, and camped the night of the 18th with
him on the Goldsboro' road, twenty-seven miles from
Goldsboro', about five miles from Bentonville, and where
the road from Clinton to Smithfield crosses the Goldsboro'
road. Howard was at Lee's Store, only two miles south,
and both columns had pickets three miles forward, to where
the two roads came together and became common to Goldsboro'.

All the signs induced me to believe that the enemy
would make no further opposition to our progress, and
would not attempt to strike us in flank while in motion.
I therefore directed Howard to move his right wing by
the new Goldsboro' road, which goes by way of Falling
Creek Church. I also left Slocum and joined Howard's
column, with a view to open communications with General
Schofield, coming up from Newbern, and Terry, from Wilmington. I found General Howard's column well strung
out, owing to the very bad roads, and did not overtake
him in person till he had reached Falling Creek Church,
with one regiment forward to the cross-roads near Cox's
Bridge across the Neuse. I had gone from General Slocum about six miles, when I heard artillery in his direction, but was soon made easy by one of his staff-officers
overtaking me, explaining that his leading division (Carlin's) had encountered a division of rebel cavalry (Dibbrell's), which he was driving easily. But soon other staff-
officers came up, reporting that he had developed near
Bentonville the whole of the rebel army, under General
Johnston himself. I sent him orders to call up the two

divisions guarding his wagon-trains, and Hazen's division of the Fifteenth Corps, still back near Lee's Store, to fight defensively until I could draw up Blair's corps, then near Mount Olive Station, and with the remaining three divisions of the Fifteenth Corps come up on Johnston's left rear from the direction of Cox's Bridge. In the mean time, while on the road, I received couriers from both Generals Schofield and Terry. The former reported himself in possession of Kinston, delayed somewhat by want of provisions, but able to march so as to make Goldsboro' on the 21st; and Terry was at or near Faison's Depot. Orders were at once dispatched to Schofield to push for Goldsboro, and to make dispositions to cross Little River in the direction of Smithfield as far as Millard; to General Terry to move to Cox's Bridge, lay a pontoon bridge, and establish a crossing; and to Blair to make a night march to Falling Creek Church; and at daylight the right wing, General Howard, less the necessary wagon guards, was put in rapid motion on Bentonville. By subsequent reports I learned that General Slocum's head of column had advanced from its camp of March 18, and first encountered Dibbrell's cavalry, but soon found his progress impeded by infantry and artillery. The enemy attacked his head of column, gaining a temporary advantage, and took three guns and caissons of General Carlin's division, driving the two leading brigades back on the main body. As soon as General Slocum realized that he had in his front the whole Confederate army, he promptly deployed the two divisions of the Fourteenth Corps, General Davis, and rapidly brought up on their left the two divisions of the Twentieth Corps, General Williams. These he arranged on the defensive, and hastily prepared a line of barricades. General Kilpatrick also came up at the sound of artillery and

massed on the left. In this position the left received six
distinct assaults by the combined forces of Hoke, Hardee,
and Cheatham, under the immediate command of General
Johnston himself, without giving an inch of ground, and
doing good execution on the enemy's ranks, especially with
our artillery, the enemy having little or none.

Johnston had moved by night from Smithfield with
great rapidity, and without unnecessary wheels, intending
to overwhelm my left flank before it could be relieved by
its co-operating columns. But he "reckoned without his
host." I had expected just such a movement all the way
from Fayetteville, and was prepared for it. During the
night of the 19th General Slocum got up his wagon-train
with its guard of two divisions, and Hazen's division of the
Fifteenth Corps, which reinforcement enabled him to make
his position impregnable. The right wing found rebel
cavalry watching his approach, but unable to offer any
serious opposition until our head of column encountered a
considerable body behind a barricade at the forks of the
road near Bentonville, about three miles east of the battle-
field of the day before. This body of cavalry was, however, quickly dislodged, and the intersection of the roads
secured. On moving forward the Fifteenth Corps, General
Logan found that the enemy had thrown back his left
flank, and had constructed a line of parapet connecting
with that towards General Slocum, in the form of a bastion,
its salient on the main Goldsboro' road, interposing
between General Slocum on the west and General Howard
on the east, while the flanks rested on Mill Creek, covering
the road back to Smithfield. General Howard was instructed to proceed with due caution until he had made
strong connection on his left with General Slocum. This
he soon accomplished, and by 4 p. m. of the 20th a com-

plete and strong line of battle confronted the enemy in his
intrenched position, and General Johnston, instead of
catching us in detail, was on the defensive, with Mill Creek
and a single bridge to his rear. Nevertheless, we had no
object to accomplish by a battle, unless at an advantage,
and therefore my general instructions were to press
steadily with skirmishers alone, to use artillery pretty
freely on the wooded space held by the enemy, and to feel
pretty strongly the flanks of his position, which were as
usual covered by the endless swamps of this region of
country. I also ordered all empty wagons to be sent at
once to Kinston for supplies, and other impediments to be
grouped near the Neuse, south of Goldsboro', holding the
real army in close contact with the enemy, ready to fight
him if he ventured outside his parapets and swampy obstructions. Thus matters stood about Bentonville on the 21st
of March. On the same day General Schofield entered
Goldsboro' with little or no opposition, and General Terry
had got possession of the Neuse River at Cox's Bridge, ten
miles above, with a pontoon bridge laid and a brigade
across, so that the three armies were in actual connection,
and the great object of the campaign was accomplished.

On the 21st a steady rain prevailed, during which General Mower's division of the Seventeenth Corps, on the
extreme right, had worked well to the right around the
enemy's flank, and had nearly reached the bridge across
Mill Creek, the only line of retreat open to the enemy. Of
course there was extreme danger that the enemy would
turn on him all his reserves, and, it might be, let go his parapets to overwhelm Mower. Accordingly I ordered at
once a general attack by our skirmish-line from left to
right. Quite a noisy battle ensued, during which General
Mower was enabled to regain his connection with his own

corps by moving to his left rear. Still he had developed a weakness in the enemy's position, of which advantage might have been taken; but that night the enemy retreated on Smithfield, leaving his pickets to fall into our hands, with many dead unburied, and wounded in his field-hospitals. At daybreak of the 22d, pursuit was made two miles beyond Mill Creek, but checked by my order. General Johnston had utterly failed in his attempt, and we remained in full possession of the field of battle.

General Slocum reports the losses of the left wing about Bentonville at 9 officers and 145 men killed, 51 officers and 816 men wounded, and 3 officers and 223 men missing, taken prisoners by the enemy; total, 1,247. He buried on the field 167 rebel dead, and took 338 prisoners. General Howard reports the losses of the right wing at 2 officers and 35 men killed, 12 officers and 239 men wounded, and 1 officer and 60 men missing; total, 399. He also buried 100 rebel dead, and took 1,287 prisoners. The cavalry of Kilpatrick was held in reserve, and lost but few, if any, of which I have no report as yet. Our aggregate loss at Bentonville was 1,643. I am well satisfied that the enemy lost heavily, especially during his assaults on the left wing during the afternoon of the 19th; but as I have no data save his dead and wounded left in our hands, I prefer to make no comparisons. Thus, as I have endeavored to explain, we had completed our march on the 21st, and had full possession of Goldsboro', the real "objective," with its two railroads back to the seaports of Wilmington and Beaufort, North Carolina. These were being rapidly repaired by strong working-parties directed by Colonel W. W. Wright, of the railroad department. A large number of supplies had already been brought forward to Kinston, to which place our wagons had been sent to

receive them.   I therefore directed General Howard and
the cavalry to remain at Bentonville, during the 22d, to
bury the dead and remove the wounded, and on the following day all the armies to move to the camps assigned
them about Goldsboro', there to rest and receive the clothing and supplies of which they stood in need.   In person I
went on the 23d to Cox's Bridge to meet General Terry,
whom I met for the first time, and on the following day
rode into Goldsboro', where I found General Schofield and
his army.   The left wing came in during the same day and
next morning, and the right wing followed on the 24th, on
which day the cavalry moved to Mount Olive Station, and
General Terry back to Faison's.   On the 25th, the Newbern Railroad was finished, and the first train of cars came
in, thus giving us the means of bringing from the depot at
Morehead City full supplies to the army.

It was all-important that I should have an interview with
the general-in-chief, and presuming that he could not at
this time leave City Point, I left General Schofield in chief
command, and proceeded with all expedition by rail to
Morehead City, and thence by steamer to City Point,
reaching General Grant's headquarters on the evening of
the 27th of March.   I had the good fortune to meet General Grant, the President, Generals Meade, Ord, and
others of the Army of the Potomac, and soon learned the
general state of the military world, from which I had been
in a great measure cut off since January.   Having completed all necessary business, I re-embarked on the navy
steamer Bat, Captain Barnes, which Admiral Porter placed
at my command, and returned *via* Hatteras Inlet and
Newbern, reaching my own headquarters in Goldsboro'
during the night of the 30th.   During my absence full
supplies of clothing and food had been brought to camp,

and all things were working well. I have thus rapidly sketched the progress of our columns from Savannah to Goldsboro', but for more minute details must refer to the reports of subordinate commanders and of staff-officers, which are not yet ready, but will in due season be forwarded and filed with this report. I cannot even, with any degree of precision, recapitulate the vast amount of injury done to the enemy, or the quantity of guns and materials of war captured and destroyed. In general terms, we have traversed the country from Savannah to Goldsboro', with an average breadth of forty miles, consuming all the forage, cattle, hogs, sheep, poultry, cured meats, corn-meal, etc. The public enemy, instead of drawing supplies from that region to feed his armies, will be compelled to send provisions from other quarters to feed the inhabitants. A map herewith, prepared by my chief engineer, Colonel Poe, with the routes of the Fourth Corps and cavalry, will show at a glance the country traversed. Of course the abandonment to us by the enemy of the whole seacoast, from Savannah to Newbern, North Carolina, with its forts, dock-yards, gunboats, etc., was a necessary incident to our occupation and destruction of the inland routes of travel and supply. But the real object of this march was to place this army in a position easy of supply, whence it could take an appropriate part in the spring and summer campaign of 1865. This was completely accomplished on March 21st by the junction of the three armies and occupation of Goldsboro'.

In conclusion, I beg to express in the most emphatic manner my entire satisfaction with the tone and temper of the whole army. Nothing seems to dampen their energy, zeal, or cheerfulness. It is impossible to conceive a march involving more labor and exposure, yet I cannot recall an instance of bad temper by the way, or hearing an expression of doubt as to our perfect success in the end. I believe that this cheerfulness and harmony of action reflects upon all concerned quite as much real honor and fame as "battles gained" or "cities won," and I therefore commend all, general, staff, officers, and men, for these high qualities, in addition to the more soldierly ones of obedience to orders and the alacrity they have always manifested when danger summoned them "to the front."

I have the honor to be, your obedient servant,

W. T. SHERMAN,
Major-General commanding.

Major-General H. W. HALLECK,
Chief of Staff, Washington, D. C

IV.

THE CLOSE OF THE CAMPAIGN,

AND THE SURRENDER OF THE CONFEDERATE FORCES UNDER GENERAL JOSEPH E. JOHNSTON;

With General Sherman's Farewell Address to his Army.

HEADQUARTERS MILITARY DIVISION OF THE MISSISSIPPI,
In the Field, City Point, Va., May 9, 1865.

GENERAL—My last official report brought the history of events, as connected with the armies in the field subject to my immediate command, down to the 1st of April, when the Army of the Ohio, Major-General J. M. Schofield commanding, lay at Goldsboro', with detachments distributed so as to secure and cover our routes of communication and supply back to the sea at Wilmington and Morehead City; Major-General A. H. Terry, with the Tenth Corps, being at Faison's Depot. The Army of the Tennessee, Major-General O. O. Howard commanding, was encamped to the right and front of Goldsboro', and the Army of Georgia, Major-General H. W. Slocum commanding, to its left and front; the cavalry, brevet Major-General J. Kilpatrick commanding, at Mount Olive. All were busy in repairing the wear and tear of our then recent and hard march from Savannah, or in replenishing clothing and stores necessary for a further progress.

I had previously, by letter and in person, notified the
lieutenant-general commanding the armies of the United
States, that the 10th of April would be the earliest possible moment at which I could hope to have all things in
readiness, and we were compelled to use our railroads to
the very highest possible limit in order to fulfil that
promise. Owing to a mistake in the railroad department,
in sending locomotives and cars of the five-foot gauge, we
were limited to the use of a few locomotives and cars of
the four-foot eight-and-a-half-inch gauge already in North
Carolina, with such of the old stock as was captured by
Major-General Terry at Wilmington, and on his way up
to Goldsboro'. Yet such judicious use was made of these,
and such industry displayed in the railroad management
by Generals Eaton and Beckwith, and Colonel Wright and
Mr. Van Dyne, that by the 10th of April our men were
all reclad, the wagons reloaded, and a fair amout of forage
accumulated ahead.

In the mean time, Major-General George Stoneman, in
command of a division of cavalry, operating from East
Tennessee in connection with Major-General George H.
Thomas, in pursuance of my orders of January 21, 1865,
had reached the railroad about Greensboro', North Carolina,
and had made sad havoc with it, and had pushed along it
to Salisbury, destroying *en route* bridges, culverts, depots,
and all kinds of rebel supplies; and had extended the
break in the railroad down to the Catawba Bridge.

This was fatal to the hostile armies of Lee and Johnston,
who depended on that road for supplies and as their ulti-
mate line of retreat. Major-General J. H. Wilson, also in
command of the cavalry corps organized by himself, under
Special Field Orders, No.——, of October 24, 1864, at Gaylesville, Alabama, had started from the neighborhood of De-

catur and Florence, Alabama, and moved straight into the heart of Alabama, on a route prescribed for General Thomas after he had defeated General Hood at Nashville, Tennessee; but the roads being too heavy for infantry, General Thomas had devolved that duty on that most energetic young cavalry officer, General Wilson, who, imbued with the proper spirit, has struck one of the best blows of the war at the waning strength of the Confederacy. His route was one never before touched by our troops, and afforded him abundance of supplies as long as he was in motion, viz., by Tuscaloosa, Selma, Montgomery, Columbus, and Macon. Though in communication with him, I have not been able to receive as yet his full and detailed reports, which will in due time be published and appreciated.

Lieutenant-General Grant, also in immediate command of the armies about Richmond, had taken the initiative in that magnificent campaign, which in less than ten days compelled the evacuation of Richmond, and resulted in the destruction and surrender of the entire rebel Army of Virginia, under command of General Lee. The news of the battles about Petersburg reached me at Goldsboro' on the 6th of April. Up to that time my purpose was to move rapidly northward, feigning on Raleigh, and striking straight for Burkesville, thereby interposing between Johnston and Lee. But the auspicious events in Virginia had changed the whole military problem, and, in the expressive language of Lieutenant-General Grant, the Confederate armies of Lee and Johnston became the strategic points. General Grant was fully able to take care of the former, and my task was to capture or destroy the latter. Johnston at that time, April 6, had his army well in hand about Smithfield, interposing between me and Raleigh. I estimated his infantry and artillery at 35,000, and his cavalry from 6,000 to 10,000. He was superior to me in cavalry, so that I held General Kilpatrick in reserve at Mount Olive, with orders to recruit his horses and be ready to make a sudden and rapid march on the 10th of April.

At daybreak on the day appointed all the heads of columns were in motion straight against the enemy, Major-General H. W. Slocum taking the two direct roads for Smithfield; Major-General O. O. Howard making a circuit by the right, and feigning up the Weldon road to disconcert the enemy's cavalry; Generals Terry and Kilpatrick moving on the west side of the Neuse River, and aiming to reach the rear of the enemy between Smithfield and Raleigh. General Schofield followed General Slocum in support. All the columns met within six (6) miles of Goldsboro', more or less cavalry, with the usual rail-barricades, which were swept before us as chaff; and by 10 A.M. of the 11th the Fourteenth Corps entered Smithfield, the Twentieth Corps close at hand. Johnston had rapidly retreated across the Neuse River, and having his railroad to lighten up his trains, could retreat faster than we could pursue. The rains had also set in, making the resort to corduroy absolutely necessary to pass even ambulances. The enemy had burned the bridge at Smithfield, and as soon as possible Major-General Slocum got up his pontoons and crossed over a division of the Fourteenth Corps. We there heard of the surrender of Lee's army at Appomattox Court-house, Virginia, which was announced to the armies in orders, and created universal joy. Not an officer or soldier of my armies but expressed a pride and satisfaction that it fell to the lot of the armies of the Potomac and James so gloriously to overwhelm and capture the entire army that had held them so long in check, and their success gave new impulse to finish up our task.

Without a moment's hesitation we dropped our trains, and marched rapidly in pursuit to and through Raleigh, reaching that place at 7.30 A. M. on the 13th, in a heavy rain. The next day the cavalry pushed on through the rain to Durham's Station, the Fifteenth Corps following as far as Morrisville Station, and the Seventeenth Corps to Jones's Station. On the supposition that Johnston was tied to his railroad, as a line of retreat by Hillsboro', Greenboro', Salisbury, and Charlotte, etc., I had turned the other columns across the bend in that road towards Ashboro'. (See Special Field Orders, No. 55.) The cavalry, brevet Major-General J. Kilpatrick commanding, was ordered to keep up a show of pursuit towards the " Company's Shops" in Alamance County; Major-General O. O. Howard to turn to the left by Hackney's Cross-roads, Pittsboro', St. Lawrence, and Ashboro'; Major-General H. W. Slocum to cross Cape Fear River at Avon's Ferry, and move rapidly by Carthage, Caledonia, and Cox's mills. Major-General J. M. Schofield was to hold Raleigh, and the road back, and with his spare force to follow an intermediate route.

By the 15th, though the rains were incessant and the roads almost impracticable, Major-General Slocum had the Fourteenth Corps, brevet Major-General Davis commanding, near Martha's Vineyard, with a pontoon bridge laid across Cape Fear River at Avon's Ferry, with the Twentieth Corps, Major-General Mower commanding, in support; and Major-General Howard had the Fifteenth and Seventeenth Corps stretched out on the roads towards Pittsboro'; while General Kilpatrick held Durham's Station and Chapel Hill University. Johnston's army was retreating rapidly on the roads from Hillsboro' to Greensboro', he himself at Greensboro'.

Although out of place as to time. I here invite all military critics, who study the problems of war, to take their maps and compare the position of my army on the 15th and 16th of April with that of General Halleck about Burkesville and Petersburg, Virginia, on the 26th of April, when, according to his telegram to Secretary Stanton,[*] he offered to relieve me of the task of cutting off Johnston's retreat. Major-General Stoneman at the time was at Statesville, and Johnston's only line of retreat was by Salisbury and Charlotte. It may be that General Halleck's troops can outmarch mine, but there is nothing in their past history to show it. Or it may be that General Halleck can inspire his troops with more energy of action. I doubt that also, save and except in this single instance, when he knew the enemy was ready to surrender or "disperse," as advised by my letter of April 18, addressed to him when chief of staff at Washington city, and delivered at Washington on the 21st instant by Major Hitchcock of my staff.

Thus matters stood at the time I received General Johnston's first letter and made my answer of April 14, copies of which were sent with all expedition to Lieutenant-General Grant and the Secretary of War, with my letter of April 15.[†] I agreed to meet General Johnston in person, at a point intermediate between our pickets, on the 17th, at noon, provided the position of the troops remained *in statu quo*. I was both willing and anxious thus to consume a few days, as it would enable Colonel Wright to finish our railroad to Raleigh. Two bridges had to be built and twelve miles of new road made. We had no iron, except by taking up that on the branch from Goldsboro' to Wel-

---

[*] This dispatch will be found in the concluding chapter of the present work.

[†] The correspondence appears in full on page 137, *et seq.*

don. Instead of losing by time, I gained in every way, for every hour of delay possible was required to reconstruct the railroad to our rear, and improve the condition of our wagon-roads to the front, so desirable in case the negotiations failed, and we be forced to make the race of near two hundred miles to head off or catch Johnston's army, then retreating towards Charlotte.

At noon of the day appointed I met General Johnston for the first time in my life, although we had been exchanging shots constantly since May, 1863. Our interview was frank and soldier-like, and he gave me to understand that further war on the part of the Confederate troops was folly; that the "cause" was lost, and that every life sacrificed after the surrender of Lee's army was the highest possible crime. He admitted that the terms conceded to General Lee were magnanimous, and all he could ask; but he did want some general concessions that would enable him to allay the natural fears and anxieties of his followers, and enable him to maintain his control over them until they could be got back to the neighborhood of their homes, thereby saving the State of North Carolina the devastation inevitably to result from turning his men loose and unprovided on the spot, and our pursuit across the State.

He also wanted to embrace in the same general proposition the fate of all the Confederate armies that remained in existence. I never made any concession as to his own army, or assumed to deal finally and authoritatively in regard to any other; but it did seem to me that there was presented a chance for peace that might be deemed valuable to the Government of the United States, and was at least worth the few days that would be consumed in reference.

To push an enemy whose commander had so frankly and

honestly confessed his inability to cope with me, were cowardly, and unworthy the brave men I led.

Inasmuch as General Johnston did not feel authorized to pledge his power over the armies in Texas, we adjourned to meet the next day at noon. I returned to Raleigh, and conferred freely with all my general officers, *every one* o whom urged me to conclude terms that might accomplish so complete and desirable an end. All dreaded the weary and laborious march after a fugitive and dissolving army back towards Georgia, almost over the very country where we had toiled so long. There was but one opinion expressed, and if contrary ones were entertained they were withheld, or indulged in only by that class who shun the fight and the march, but are loudest, bravest, and fiercest when danger is past.

I again met General Johnston on the 18th, and we renewed the conversation. He satisfied me then of his *power* to disband the rebel armies in Alabama, Mississippi, Louisiana, and Texas, as well as those in his immediate command, viz., North Carolina, South Carolina, Florida, and Georgia. The points on which he expressed especial solicitude were lest their States were to be dismembered and denied representation in Congress, or any separate political existence whatever ; and that the absolute disarming his men would leave the South powerless and exposed to depredations by wicked bands of assassins and robbers.

President Lincoln's message of 1864 ; his amnesty proclamation ; General Grant's terms to General Lee, substantially extending the benefits of that proclamation to all officers above the rank of colonel ; the invitation to the Virginia Legislature to reassemble in Richmond, by General Weitzel,*

---

* Given at the end of this volume

with the approval of Mr. Lincoln and General Grant, then on the spot; a firm belief that I had been fighting to re-establish the Constitution of the United States ; and last, and not least, the general and universal desire to close a war any longer without organized resistance, were the leading facts that induced me to pen the "memorandum" of April 18, signed by myself and General Johnston. It was designed to be, and so expressed on its face, as a mere "basis" for reference to the President of the United States and constitutional commander-in-chief, to enable him, if he chose, at one blow to dissipate the military power of the Confederacy, which had threatened the national safety for years. It admitted of modification, alteration, and change. It had no appearance of an ultimatum, and by no false reasoning can it be construed into a usurpation of power on my part. I have my opinions on the question involved, and will stand by the memorandum. "But this forms no part of a military report."

Immediately on my return to Raleigh I dispatched one of my staff, Major Hitchcock, to Washington, enjoining him to be most prudent, and careful to avoid the spies and informers that would be sure to infest him by the way, and to say nothing to anybody until the President could make known to me his wishes and policy in the matter.

The news of President Lincoln's assassination, on the 14th of April (wrongly reported to me by telegraph as having occurred on the 11th), reached me on the 17th, and was announced to my command on the same day, in Special Field Orders, No. 56. I was duly impressed with its horrible atrocity and probable effect on the country. But when the property and interests of millions still living were involved, I saw no good reason to change my course, but thought rather to manifest real respect for his memory by following, after his death, that policy which, if living, I feel certain he would have approved, or at least not rejected with disdain.

Up to that hour I had never received one word of instruction, advice, or counsel, as to the plan or policy of Government, looking to a restoration of peace on the part of the rebel States of the South. Whenever asked for an opinion on the points involved, I had always evaded the subject. My letter to the Mayor of Atlanta has been published to the world, and I was not rebuked by the War Department for it.

My letter to Mr. N—— W——, at Savannah, was shown by me to Mr. Stanton, before its publication, and all that my memory retains of his answer is that he said, like my letters generally, it was sufficiently emphatic and could not be misunderstood.

But these letters asserted my belief that according to Mr. Lincoln's proclamations and messages, when the people of the South had laid down their arms and submitted to the lawful power of the United States, *ipso facto*, the war was over as to them; and furthermore, that if any State in rebellion would conform to the Constitution of the United States, cease war, elect senators and representatives to Congress, if admitted (of which each house of Congress alone is the judge), that State becomes instanter as much in the Union as New York or Ohio. Nor was I rebuked for this expression, though it was universally known and commented on at the time. And again Mr. Stanton, in person, at Savannah, speaking of the terrific expenses of the war, and difficulty of realizing the money necessary for the daily wants of Government, impressed me most forcibly with the necessity of bringing the war to a close as soon as possible, for *financial reasons*.

On the evening of April 23, Major Hitchcock reported his return to Morehead City with dispatches, of which fact General Johnston, at Hillsborough, was notified, so as to be ready in the morning for an answer. At 6 o'clock A. M. on the 24th, Major Hitchcock arrived, accompanied by General Grant and members of his staff, who had not telegraphed the fact of his coming over our exposed road for prudential reasons.

I soon learned that the memorandum was disapproved, without reasons assigned, and I was ordered to give the forty-eight hours' notice, and resume hostilities at the close of that time, governing myself by the substance of a dispatch then inclosed, dated March 3, 12 M., at Washington, D. C., from Secretary Stanton to General Grant at City Point; but not accompanied by any part of the voluminous matter so liberally lavished on the public in the New York journals of the 24th of April.* That was the first and only time I ever saw that telegram, or had one word of instruction on the important matters involved in it, and it does seem strange to me that every bar-room loafer in New York can read in the morning journals " official" matter that is withheld from a general whose command extends from Kentucky to North Carolina.

Within an hour a courier was riding from Durham's Station towards Hillsborough, with notice to General Johnston of the suspension of the truce, and renewing my demand for the surrender of the armies under his immediate command (see two letters of April 24, 6 A. M.); and at 12 M. I had the receipt of his picket-officer. I therefore published my Orders No. 62 to the troops, terminating the truce at 12 M. on the 26th, and ordered all to be in

---

* These will be found in the concluding chapter.

readiness to march at that hour, on the routes prescribed in Special Field Orders, No. 55, of April 14th, from the positions held April 18th.

General Grant had orders from the President, through the secretary of war, to direct military movements, and I explained to him the exact position of the troops, and he approved of it most emphatically; but he did not relieve me, or express a wish to assume command. All things were in readiness, when, on the evening of the 25th, I received another letter from General Johnston, asking another interview to renew negotiations.

General Grant not only approved, but urged me to accept, and I appointed a meeting at our former place at noon of the 26th, the very hour fixed for the renewal of hostilities. General Johnston was delayed by an accident to his train, but at 2 P. M. arrived. We then consulted, concluded and signed the final terms of capitulation.

These were taken by me back to Raleigh, submitted to General Grant, and met his immediate approval and signature. General Johnston was not even aware of the presence of General Grant at Raleigh at the time.

Thus was surrendered to us the second great army of the so-called Confederacy; and though undue importance has been given to the so-called negotiations which preceded it, and a rebuke and public disfavor cast on me wholly unwarranted by the facts, I rejoice in saying that it was accomplished without further ruin and devastation to the country; without the loss of a single life to those gallant men who had followed me from the Mississippi to the Atlantic; and without subjecting brave men to the ungracious task of pursuing a fleeing foe that did not want to fight. As for myself, I know my motives, and challenge the instance during the past four years, where an armed and defiant foe stood before me, that I did not go in for a fight, and I would blush for shame if I had ever insulted or struck a fallen foe.

The instant the terms of surrender were approved by General Grant, I made my Orders, No. 65, assigning to each of my subordinate commanders his share of the work, and, with General Grant's approval, made Special Field Orders, No. 66, putting in motion my old army, no longer required in Carolina, northward for Richmond.*

General Grant left Raleigh at 9 A. M. of the 27th; and I glory in the fact that, during his three days' stay with me, I did not detect in his language or manner one particle of abatement in the confidence, respect, and affection that have existed between us throughout all the varied events of the past war; and though we have honestly differed in opinion in other cases as well as this, still we respected each other's honest convictions. I still adhere to my then opinions, that by a few general concessions, "glittering generalities," all of which in the end *must* and will be conceded to the organized States of the South, that this day there would not be an armed battalion opposed to us within the broad area of the dominions of the United States. Robbers and assassins must, in any event, result from the disbandment of large armies; but even these should be, and could be, taken care of by the local civil authorities, without being made a charge on the national treasury.

On the evening of the 28th, having concluded all business requiring my personal attention at Raleigh, and having conferred with every army commander, and delegated to him the authority necessary for his future action, I dis-

* These orders will be found on pp. 154, 155.

patched my headquarter wagons by land along with the Seventeenth Corps, the office in charge of General Webster, from Newbern to Alexandria, Va., by sea, and in person, accompanied only by my personal staff, hastened to Savannah to direct matters in the interior of South Carolina and Georgia.

I had received, across the rebel telegraph wires, cipher dispatches from General Wilson, at Macon, to the effect that he was in receipt of my orders No. 65, and would send General Upton's division to Augusta, and General McCook's division to Tallahassee, to receive the surrender of those garrisons, take charge of the public property, and execute the paroles required by the terms of surrender. He reported a sufficiency of forage for his horses in Southwest Georgia, but asked me to send him a supply of clothing, sugar, coffee, etc., by way of Augusta, Georgia, whence he could get it by rail. I therefore went rapidly to Goldsboro' and Wilmington, reaching the latter city at 10 A. M. of the 29th, and the same day embarked for Hilton Head, in the blockade-runner Russia, Captain A. M. Smith.

I found General Q. A. Gillmore, commanding Department of the South, at Hilton Head on the evening of April 30, and ordered him to send to Augusta at once what clothing and small stores he could spare for General Wilson, and to open up a line of certain communication and supply with him at Macon. Within an hour the captured steamboats Jeff. Davis and Amazon, both adapted to the shallow and crooked navigation of the Savannah River, were being loaded, the one at Savannah and the other at Hilton Head. The former started up the river on the 1st of May, in charge of a very intelligent officer (whose name I cannot recall) and forty-eight men (all the boat could carry), with orders to occupy temporarily the United States arsenal at Augusta, and open up communication with General Wilson, at Macon, in the event that General McCook's division of cavalry was not already there. The Amazon followed next day, and General Gillmore had made the necessary orders for a brigade of infantry, to be commanded by General Molyneux, to follow by a land march to Augusta, as its permanent garrison; another brigade of infantry was ordered to occupy Orangeburg, South Carolina—the point furthest in the interior that can at present be reached by rail from the seacoast (Charleston).

On the 1st of May I went on to Savannah, where General Gillmore also joined me, and the arrangements ordered for the occupation of Augusta were consummated. At Savannah I found the city in the most admirable police, under direction of brevet Major-General Grover, and the citizens manifested the most unqualified joy to hear that, so far as they were concerned, the war was over. All classes, Union men as well as former rebels, did not conceal, however, the apprehensions naturally arising from a total ignorance of the political conditions to be attached to their future state. Any thing at all would be preferable to this dread uncertainty.

On the evening of the 2d of May I returned to Hilton Head, and there for the first time received the New York papers of April 28, containing Secretary Stanton's dispatch of 9 A. M. of the 27th of April to General Dix, including General Halleck's from Richmond of 9 P. M. the night before,* which seems to have been rushed with extreme haste before an excited public, viz., morning of the 28th. You will observe from the dates that these dispatches were

---

* Given in the concluding chapter.

running back and forth from Richmond and Washington to New York, and there published, while General Grant and I were together in Raleigh, N. C., adjusting, to the best of our ability, the terms of surrender of the only remaining formidable rebel army in existence at the time east of the Mississippi River. Not one word of intimation had been sent to me of the displeasure of the Government with my official conduct, but only the naked disapproval of a skeleton memorandum sent properly for the action of the President of the United States.

The most objectionable features of my memorandum had already (April 24) been published to the world in violation of official usage; and the contents of my accompanying letters to General Halleck, General Grant, and Mr. Stanton, of even date, though at hand, were suppressed. In all these letters I had stated clearly and distinctly that Johnston's army would not fight, but if pushed would "disband" and scatter into small and dangerous guerrilla parties, as injurious to the interests of the United States as to the rebels themselves; that all parties admitted that the rebel cause of the South was abandoned, that the negro was free, and that the temper of all was most favorable to a lasting peace. I say all these opinions of mine were withheld from the public with a seeming purpose. And I do contend that my official experience and former services, as well as my past life and familiarity with the people and geography of the South, entitle my opinions to at least a decent respect.

Although this dispatch (Mr. Stanton's, of April 27) was printed "official," it had come to me only in the questionable newspaper paragraph headed, "Sherman's truce disregarded."

I had already done what General Wilson wanted me to

do, viz., had sent him supplies of clothing and food, with clear and distinct orders and instructions how to carry out, in Western Georgia, the terms for the surrender of arms and paroling of prisoners made by General Johnston's capitulation of April 26, and had properly and most opportunely ordered General Gillmore to occupy Orangeburg and Augusta—strategic points of great value at all times, in peace or war. But as the secretary had taken upon himself to order my subordinate generals to disobey my " orders," I explained to General Gillmore that I would no longer confuse him or General Wilson with " orders" that might conflict with those of the secretary, which, as re-- ported, were not sent through me, but in open disregard of me and my lawful authority.

It now becomes my duty to paint, in justly severe character, the still more offensive and dangerous matter of General Halleck's dispatch, of April 26, to the secretary of war, embodied in his to General Dix, of April 27. General Halleck had been chief of staff of the army at Washington, in which capacity he must have received my official letter of April 18, wherein I wrote, clearly, that if Johnston's army about Greensboro' were pushed, it would " disperse"—an event I wished to prevent. About that time he seems to have been sent from Washington to Richmond to command the new military division of the James ; in assuming charge of which, on the 22d, he defines the limits of his authority to be the " Department of Virginia, the Army of the Potomac, and such part of North Carolina as may not be occupied by the command of Major-General Sherman." (See his General Orders, No. 1.) Four days later (April 26) he reports to the secretary that he has ordered Generals Meade, Sheridan, and Wright to invade that part of North Carolina which *was* occupied by my

command, and pay " no regard to any truce or orders of "
mine. They were ordered to " push forward regardless of
any order save those of Lieutenant-General Grant, and
cut off Johnston's retreat." He knew at the time he
penned that dispatch and made those orders that Johnston
was not retreating, but was halted under a forty-eight
hours' truce with me, and was laboring to surrender his
command, and prevent its dispersion into guerilla bands;
and that I had on the spot a magnificent army at my
command, amply sufficient for all purposes required by the
occasion. The plan for cutting off a retreat from the direction of Burkesville and Danville is hardly worthy of one
of his military education and genius.

When he contemplated an act so questionable as the violation of a truce made by competent authority within his
sphere of command, he should have gone himself, and not
have sent subordinates, for he knew I was bound in *honor*
to *defend and maintain* my *own* truce and pledge of faith,
even at the cost of many lives. When an officer pledges
the faith of his government he is bound to defend it, and
he is no soldier who would violate it knowingly.

As to Davis and his stolen treasure, did General Halleck,
as chief of staff or commanding officer of the neighboring
military division, notify me of the facts contained in his
dispatch to the secretary? No, he did not. If the secretary of war wanted Davis caught, why not order it, instead of, by publishing it in the newspapers, putting him on
his guard to hide away and escape? No orders or in-
stuctions to catch Davis and his stolen treasure ever came
to me, but on the contrary I was led to believe that the
secretary of war rather preferred he should effect an escape
from the country, if made " unknown" to him.

But even on this point I inclose a copy of my letter to

Admiral Dahlgren, at Charleston, sent him by a fleet steamer from Wilmington, on the 25th of April, two days before the bankers of Richmond had imparted to General Halleck the important secret as to Davis's movements, designed, doubtless, to stimulate his troops to march their legs off to catch their treasure for *their* own use. I know now that Admiral Dahlgren did receive my letter on the 26th, and had acted on it before General Halleck had even thought of the matter. But I don't believe a word of the treasure story ; it is absurd on its face, and General Halleck or anybody has my full permission to chase Jeff. Davis and cabinet, with their stolen treasure, through any part of the country occupied by my command.

The last and most obnoxious feature of General Halleck's dispatch is where he goes out of his way, and advises that my subordinates, Generals Thomas, Stoneman, and Wilson, should be instructed " not to obey Sherman's commands."

This is too much, and I turn from the subject with feelings too strong for words, and merely record my belief that so much mischief was never before embraced in so small a space as in the newspaper paragraph headed, " Sherman's truce disregarded," authenticated as " official" by Mr. Secretary Stanton, and published in the New York papers of April 28.

During the night of May 2d, at Hilton Head, having concluded my business in the department of the South, I began my return to meet my troops, then marching towards Richmond from Raleigh. On the morning of the 3d, we ran into Charleston harbor, where I had the pleasure to meet Admiral Dahlgren, who had, in all my previous operations from Savannah northward, aided me with a courtesy and manliness that commanded my entire respect and deep affection. Also General Hatch, who, from our

6*

first interview at his Tullafinnay camp, had caught the
spirit of the move from Pocotaligo northward, and had
largely contributed to our joint success in taking Charleston and the Carolina coast.   Any one who is not *satisfied*
with war, should go and see Charleston, and he will pray
louder and deeper than ever that the country may, in the
long future, be spared any more war.   Charleston and se-
cession being synonymous terms, the city should be left as
a sample, so that centuries will pass away before that false
doctrine is again preached in our Union.

We left Charleston on the evening of the 3d of May,
and hastened with all possible speed back to Morehead
City, which we reached at night on the 4th.   I immediately
communicated by telegraph to General Schofield at Raleigh, and learned from him the pleasing fact that the
lieutenant-general commanding the armies of the United
States had reached the Chesapeake in time to countermand
General Halleck's orders, and prevent his violating my truce,
invading the area of my command, and driving Johnston's
surrendering army into fragments.   General Johnston had
fulfilled his agreement to the very best of his ability, and
the officers, charged with issuing the paroles at Greensboro',
reported about thirty thousand (30,000) already made, and
that the greater part of the North Carolina troops had gone
home without waiting for their papers; but that all of
them would, doubtless, come into some one of the military
posts, the commanders of which are authorized to grant
them.   About eight hundred (800) of the rebel cavalry had
gone south, refusing to abide the terms of the surrender,
and it was supposed they would make for Mexico.   I would
sincerely advise that they be encouraged to go and stay.
They would be a nuisance to any civilized government,
whether loose or in prison.

With the exception of some plundering on the part of Lee's and Johnston's disbanded men, all else in North Carolina was quiet. When, to the number of men surrendered at Greensboro', are added those at Tallahassee, Augusta, and Macon, with the scattered squads who will come in at other military posts, I have no doubt fifty thousand (50,000) armed men will be disarmed and restored to civil pursuits, by the capitulation made near Durham's Station, North Carolina, on the 26th of April, and that, too, without the loss of a single life to us.

On the 5th of May I received, and here subjoin, a further dispatch from Gen. Schofield, which contains inquiries I have been unable to satisfy, similar to those made by nearly every officer in my command whose duty brings him in contact with citizens. I leave you to do what you think expedient to provide the military remedy.

By Telegraph from Raleigh, N. C., May 5, 1865.

To Major-General W. T. Sherman, *Morehead City.*

When General Grant was here, as you doubtless recollect, he said the lines had been extended to embrace this and other States south. The order, it seems, has been modified so as to include only Virginia and Tennessee. I think it would be an act of wisdom to open this State to trade at once. I hope the Government will make known its policy as to the organs of State government without delay. Affairs must necessarily be in a very unsettled state until that is done. The people are now in a mood to accept almost any thing which promises a definite settlement. What is to be done with the freedmen is the question of all, and it is the all-important question. It requires prompt and wise action to prevent the negro from becoming a huge elephant on our hands. If I am to govern this

State, it is important for me to know it at once. If another is to be sent here, it cannot be done too soon, for he will probably undo the most that I shall have done. I shall be glad to hear from you fully when you have time to write. I will send your message to General Wilson at once.

J. M. SCHOFIELD, Major-General.

I give this dispatch entire, to demonstrate how intermingled have become civil matters with the military, and how almost impossible it has become for an officer in authority to act a pure military part. There are no longer armed enemies in North Carolina, and a soldier can deal with no other sort. The marshals and sheriffs, with their posse (of which the military may become a part), are the only proper officers to deal with civil criminals and marauders. But I will not be drawn out into a discussion of this subject, but instance the case to show how difficult is the task become to military officers, when men of the rank, education, experience, nerve, and good sense of Gen. Schofield feel embarrassed by them.

General Schofield, at Raleigh, has a well-appointed and well-disciplined command, is in telegraphic communication with the controlling parts of his department, and the remote ones in the direction of Georgia, as well as with Washington, and has military possession of all strategic points.

In like manner, Gen. Gillmore is well situated in all respects, except as to rapid communication with the seat of the general government. I leave him also with every man he ever asked for, and in full and quiet possession of every strategic point in his department. And General Wilson has, in the very heart of Georgia, the strongest, best appointed, and best equipped cavalry corps that ever fell under my command; and he has now, by my recent action, opened to him a source and route of supply, by way of Savannah River, that simplifies his military problem; so that I think I may, with a clear conscience, leave them, and turn my attention once more to my special command—the army with which I have been associated through some of the most eventful scenes of this or any war.

I hope and believe none of these commanders will ever have reason to reproach me for any "orders" they may have received from me. And the President of the United States may be assured that all of them are in position, ready and willing to execute to the letter, and in spirit, any orders he may give. I shall henceforth cease to give them any orders at all, for the occasion that made them subordinate to me is past; and I shall confine my attention to the army composed of the Fifteenth and Seventeenth, the Fourteenth and Twentieth Corps, unless the commanding general of the armies of the United States orders otherwise.

At 4 o'clock P.M. of May 9, I reached Manchester, on the James River, opposite Richmond, and found that all the four corps had arrived from Raleigh, and were engaged in replenishing their wagons for the resumption of the march towards Alexandria.

I have the honor to be your obedient servant,

W. T. SHERMAN,
Major-General commanding.

General JOHN A. RAWLINGS,
Chief of Staff, Washington, D. C.

GENERAL SHERMAN'S FAREWELL ADDRESS TO HIS ARMY.

SPECIAL FIELD ORDERS—NO. 76.

HEADQUARTERS MILITARY DIVISION OF THE MISSISSIPPI,
In the Field, Washington, D. C., May 30, 1865.

THE general commanding announces to the Armies of the Tennessee and Georgia that the time has come for us to part. Our work is done, and armed enemies no longer defy us. Some of you will be retained in service until further orders. And now that we are about to separate, to mingle with the civil world, it becomes a pleasing duty to recall to mind the situation of national affairs when, but a little more than a year ago, we were gathered about the twining cliffs of Lookout Mountain, and all the future was wrapped in doubt and uncertainty. Three armies had come together from distant fields, with separate histories, yet bound by one common cause—the union of our country and the perpetuation of the Government of our inheritance. There is no need to recall to your memories Tunnell Hill, with its Rocky Face Mountain, and Buzzard Roost Gap, with the ugly forts of Dalton behind. We were in earnest, and paused not for danger and difficulty, but dashed through Snake Creek Gap, and fell on Resaca, then on to the Etowah, to Dallas, Kenesaw; and the heats of summer found us on the banks of the Chattahoochie, far from home and dependent on a single road for supplies. Again we were not to be held back by any obstacle, and crossed over and fought four heavy battles for the possession of the citadel of Atlanta. That was the crisis of our history. A doubt still clouded our future; but we solved the problem, and destroyed Atlanta, struck boldly across the State of Georgia, secured all the main arteries of life to our enemy, and Christmas found us at Savannah. Waiting there only long enough to fill our wagons, we again began a march, which for peril, labor, and results, will compare with any ever made by an organized army. The floods of the Savannah, the swamps of the Combahee and Edisto, the high hills and rocks of the Santee, the flat quagmires of the Pedee and Cape Fear rivers, were all passed in midwinter, with its floods and rains, in the face of an accumulating enemy; and after the battles of Averasboro' and Bentonville we once more came out of the wilderness to meet our friends at Goldsboro'. Even then we paused only long enough to get new clothing, to reload our wagons, and again pushed on to Raleigh, and beyond, until we met our enemy, sueing for peace instead of war, and offering to submit to the injured laws of his and our country. As long as that enemy was defiant, nor mountains, nor rivers, nor swamps, nor hunger, nor cold had checked us; but when he who had fought us hard and persistently offered submission, your general thought it wrong to pursue him further, and negotiations followed which resulted, as you all know, in his surrender. How far the operations of the army have contributed to the overthrow of the Confederacy, of the peace which now dawns on us, must be judged by others, not by us. But that you have done all that men could do has been admitted by those in authority; and we have a right to join in the universal joy that fills our land because the war is over, and our Government stands vindicated before the world by the joint action of the volunteer armies of the United States.

To such as remain in the military service, your general need only remind you that successes in the past are due to hard work and discipline, and that the same work and discipline are equally 'important in the future. To such as go home, he will only say, that our favored country is so grand, so extensive, so diversified in climate, soil, and productions, that every man may surely find a home and occupation suited to his taste; and none' should yield to the natural impotence sure to result from our past life of excitement and adventure. You will be invited to seek new adventure' abroad; but do not yield to the temptation, for it will lead only to death and disappointment.

Your general now bids you all farewell, with the full belief that, as in war you have been good soldiers, so in peace you will make good citizens; and if, unfortunately, new war should arise in our country, Sherman's army will be the first to buckle on the old armor and come forth to defend and maintain the Government of our inheritance and choice.

By order of

MAJOR-GENERAL W. T. SHERMAN.

L. M. DAYTON, Assistant Adjutant-General.

OFFICIAL RECORD OF THE CORRESPONDENCE

RELATING TO THE SURRENDER OF THE CONFEDERATE ARMY UN-
DER THE COMMAND OF GENERAL JOSEPH E. JOHNSTON ;

With General Sherman's Orders on Peace.

HEADQUARTERS IN THE FIELD, April 14, 1865.

Major-General W. T. SHERMAN, *Commanding United States Forces :*

GENERAL—The results of the recent campaigns in Virginia have changed the relative military condition of the
belligerents. I am therefore induced to address you, in
this form, the inquiry whether, in order to stop the further
effusion of blood and devastation of property, you are
willing to make a temporary suspension of active operations, and to communicate to Lieutenant-General Grant,
commanding the armies of the United States, the request
that he will take like action in regard to other armies, the
object being to permit the civil authorities to enter into
the needful arrangements to terminate the existing war.

I have the honor to be, very respectfully,

.   Your obedient servant,

J. E. JOHNSTON, General.

HEADQUARTERS, MILITARY DIVISION OF THE MISSISSIPPI,
In the Field, Raleigh, N. C., April 14, 1865.

General J. E. JOHNSTON, *Commanding Confederate Army :*

GENERAL—I have this moment received your communication of this date. . I am fully empowered to arrange with

you any terms for the suspension of further hostilities, as between the armies commanded by you and those commanded by myself, and will be willing to confer with you to that end. I will limit the advance of my main column, to-morrow, to Morrisville, and the cavalry to the University, and expect that you will also maintain the present position of your forces until each has notice of a failure to agree.

That a basis of action may be had, I undertake to abide by the same terms and conditions as were made by Generals Grant and Lee, at Appomattox Court-house, of the 9th instant, relative to our two armies; and, furthermore, to obtain from General Grant an order to suspend the movements of any troops from the direction of Virginia. General Stoneman is under my command, and my order will suspend any devastation or destruction contemplated by him. I will add, that I really desire to save the people of North Carolina the damage they would sustain by the march of this army through the central or western parts of the State.

I am, with respect,

Your obedient servant,

W. T. SHERMAN, Major-General.

DURHAM'S STATION, April 16, 1865.

Major-General SHERMAN :

The following dispatch has just been received from Lieutenant-General Wade Hampton.

J. KILPATRICK, Brevet Major-General.

Major-General J. KILPATRICK, *United States :*

GENERAL—The General commanding directs me to arrange for a meeting between himself and Major-General Sherman. In accordance with these instructions, I beg to inquire when and where this meeting can most conveniently be had. I suggest ten (10) o'clock A. M. to-morrow, as the hour, and a point on the Hillsboro' road, equidistant from the picket of your command and my own, as the place for the proposed meeting.

I am, respectfully, yours,

NED WADE HAMPTON, Lieutenant-General.

[The "memorandum" of agreement made April 18, between Generals Sherman and Johnston, will be found in the last chapter.]

GREENSBORO', April 19, 1865.

Major-General W. T. SHERMAN, *Commanding United States Forces in North Carolina :*

GENERAL—As your troops are moving from the coast towards the interior of South Carolina, and from Columbus towards Macon, Ga., I respectfully suggest that you send copies of your orders announcing the suspension of hostilities for transmittal to them, supposing the interior route to be the shortest.

Most respectfully, your obedient servant,

J. E. JOHNSTON, General C. S. A.

HEADQUARTERS MILITARY DIVISION OF THE MISSISSIPPI, In the Field, Raleigh, N. C., April 20, 1865.

General J. E. JOHNSTON, *Greensboro' :*

GENERAL—At your request I send you, by Major Saunders, several written and printed copies of an order I have made to this army, which announces the cessation of hostilities, etc. I dispatched a steamer from Morehead City, yesterday, for Charleston, with orders to General Gillmore to cease all acts of destruction, public or private, and to draw Generals Hatch and Potter back of the frontier. Also, by 11.30 A. M. yesterday, Major Hitchcock was on a fleet steamer at Morehead City, carrying a request to General Meade to check the movement of his army on Danville and Weldon; so that I hope your people will be spared in the Carolinas. But I am apprehensive of Wilson, who is impetuous and rapid. If you will send by telegraph and courier a single word, he will stop, and then the inclosed order will place his command at a point convenient to our supplies.

I send you a late paper, showing that in Virginia the State authorities are acknowledged and invited to resume their lawful functions.

Yours, with respect,

W. T. Sherman, Major-General.

[Telegram.]

Headquarters Army of Tennessee,
April 21, 1865—9.30 A. M.

To Lieutenant-General HAMPTON :

Transmit to General Sherman the following dispatch, dated Headquarters Cavalry Corps, Military Division of the West, Macon, Georgia, April 20, 1865.

" *To Major-General* W. T. SHERMAN, *through headquarters of General* BEAUREGARD:

" My advance received the surrender of this city with its garrison this evening. General Cobb had previously sent me, under flag of truce, a copy of the telegram from General Beauregard, declaring the existence of an armistice between all the troops under your command and those of General Johnston. Without questioning the authority of this dispatch, or its application to my command, I could not communicate orders in time to prevent the capture. I shall therefore hold the garrison, including Major-Generals Cobb and G. W. Smith, and Brigadier-General McCall, prisoners of war.

" Please send me orders. I shall remain here a reasonable length of time to hear from you.

" J. H. WILSON,

" Brevet Major-General U. S. A."

J. E. JOHNSTON, General.

Official : H. B. McCLELLAN, A. A. G.

[Telegram.]

HEADQUARTERS ARMY OF TENNESSEE,
April 21, 1865—9.30 A. M.

Major-General W. T. SHERMAN, *care Lieutenant-General* HAMPTON, *via Hillsboro' :*

I transmit a dispatch, just received by telegraph from Major-General Wilson, United States Army. Should you desire to give the orders asked for in the same manner, I beg you to send them to me through Lieutenant-General Hampton's office.

I hope that, for the sake of expedition, you are willing to take this course. I also send, for your information, a copy of a dispatch received from Major-General Cobb.

J. E. JOHNSTON.

Official : H. B. McCLELLAN, A. A. G.

[Telegram.]

HEADQUARTERS ARMY OF TENNESSEE,
April 21, 1865—9.30 A. M.

To Lieutenant General HAMPTON :

Transmit to General Sherman the following dispatch, dated Macon, Georgia, April 20.

" *To General* G. T. BEAUREGARD :

" On receipt of your dispatch at 11 o'clock to-day, I sent a flag of truce to General Wilson, with copy of the same, and informing him that I had issued orders to carry out armistice, desisting from military operations. The flag met the advance fourteen miles from the city. Before hearing from it the advance moved on the city, and having moved my picket, were in the city before I was aware of their approach.

" An unconditional surrender was demanded, to which I was forced to submit, under protest. General Wilson has since arrived, and holds the city and garrison as captured, notwithstanding my protest. He informs me he will remain in his present position a reasonable length of time to hear from his dispatch to General Sherman, sent to your care.

"HOWELL COBB, Major-General."

J. E. JOHNSTON, General.

Official : H. B. McCLELLAN, A. A. G.

_____

HEADQUARTERS MILITARY DIVISION OF THE MISSISSIPPI,
In the Field, Raleigh, N. C., April 21, 1865.

General J. E. JOHNSTON, *Commanding Confederate Army :*

GENERAL—I send you a letter for General Wilson, which, if sent by telegraph and courier, will check his career. He may distrust the telegraph, therefore better send the original, for he cannot mistake my handwriting, with which he is familiar. He seems to have his blood up, and will be hard to hold. If he can buy corn, fodder, and rations down about Fort Valley, it will obviate the necessity of his going up to Rome or Dalton.

It is reported to me from Cairo that Mobile is in our possession, but it is not minute or official.

General Baker sent in to me, wanting to surrender his command, on the theory that the whole confederate army was surrendered. I explained to him, or his staff-officer, the exact truth, and left him to act as he thought proper. He seems to have disbanded his men, deposited a few arms about twenty miles from here, and himself awaits your action. I will not hold him, his men, or arms subject to any condition other than the final one we may agree on.

I shall look for Major Hitchcock back from Washington on Wednesday, and shall promptly notify you of the result. By the action of General Weitzel in relation to the Virginia Legislature, I feel certain we will have no trouble on the score of recognizing existing State governments.* It may be the lawyers will want us to define more minutely what is meant by the guarantee of rights of person and property. It may be construed into a compact for us to undo the past as to the rights of slaves and "leases of plantations" on the Mississippi, of "vacant and abandoned" plantations. I wish you would talk to the best men you have on these points; and, if possible, let us in our final convention make these points so clear as to leave no room for angry controversy.

I believe if the South would simply and publicly declare what we all feel, that slavery is dead, that you

---

* President Lincoln's letter authorizing, and the proclamation for the assembling of the Virginia Legislature, are given at the end of this volume.

would inaugurate an era of peace and prosperity that would soon efface the ravages of the past four years of war. Negroes would remain in the South, and afford you abundance of cheap labor, which otherwise will be driven away; arfd it will save the country the senseless discussions which have kept us all in hot water for fifty years.

Although, strictly speaking, this is no subject of a military convention, yet I am honestly convinced that our simple declaration of a result will be accepted as good law everywhere. Of course, I have not a single word from Washington on this or any other point of our agreement, but I know the effect of such a step by us will be universally accepted.

I am, with great respect, your obedient servant,

W. T. SHERMAN, Major-Gen. U. S. A.

[By telegraph, through General J. E. Johnston.]

HEADQUARTERS MILITARY DIVISION OF THE MISSISSIPPI,
In the Field, Raleigh, N. C., April 21, 1865.

General JAMES H. WILSON, *Commanding Cavalry Division Mississippi—Macon, Ga.*:

GENERAL—A suspension of hostilities was agreed on between General Johnston and myself, on Tuesday, April 18, at 12 noon. I want that agreement religiously observed, and you may release the generals captured at Macon. Occupy ground convenient, and contract for supplies for your command, and forbear any act of hostility until you hear or have reason to believe hostilities are resumed. In the mean time it is also agreed·the position of the enemy must not be altered to our prejudice.

You know by this time that General Lee has surrendered to General Grant the rebel army of Northern Virginia,

and that I only await the sanction of the President to conclude terms of peace coextensive with the boundaries of the
United States. You will shape your conduct on this knowledge, unless you have overwhelming proof to the contrary.

W. T. SHERMAN,
Major-General commanding.

After the above is telegraphed, this original should be
sent to General Wilson as rapidly as possible.

W. T. SHERMAN, Major-General.

HEADQUARTERS CAVALRY CORPS, MILITARY DIVISION
OF THE MISSISSIPPI, Macon, Ga., April 21, 1864.

Major-General W. T. SHERMAN, *through General* JOHNSTON:

Your dispatch of yesterday is received. I shall at once
proceed to carry out your instructions. If proper arrangements can be made to have sugar, coffee, and clothing sent
from Savannah to Augusta, they can be brought thither by
the way of Atlanta by railroad, or they can be sent by boat
directly to this place from Darien. I shall be able to get
forage, bread, and meat from Southeastern Georgia. The
railroad from Atlanta to Dalton or Cleveland cannot be
repaired in three months. I have arranged to send an
officer at once, *via* Eufala, to General Canby, with a copy
of your dispatch. General Cobb will also notify General
Taylor of the armistice. I have about 3,000 prisoners of
war, including Generals Cobb, Smith, McCall, Mercer, and
Robertson. Can you arrange with General Johnston for
their immediate release? Please answer at once. I shall
start a staff-officer to you to-morrow.

J. H. WILSON,
Major-General Brevet commanding.

7

[Telegram.]

HEADQUARTERS ARMY OF TENNESSEE,
April 22, 1865—2.30 P. M.

Major-General W. T. SHERMAN, *Commanding U. S. Forces, Raleigh, N. C.:*

Your telegram to brevet Major-General Wilson is just received. I respectfully suggest that the sentence: "In the mean time it is also agreed that the position of the enemy's forces must not be altered to our prejudice," be so modified as to read: "In the mean time it is also agreed that the position of the forces of neither belligerent shall be altered to the prejudice of the other;" and that on this principle you direct Major-General Wilson to withdraw from Macon and release its garrison.

J. E. JOHNSTON, General.

Official: H. B. McCLELLAN, A. A. G.

————

HEADQUARTERS MILITARY DIVISION OF THE MISSISSIPPI,
In the Field, Raleigh, N. C., April 23, 1865.

General JOSEPH E. JOHNSTON, *Commanding Confederate Army, Greensboro':*

GENERAL.—Your communication of 2.20 P. M. of yesterday is received. My line of communication with General Wilson is not secure enough for me to confuse him by a change in mere words. Of course the *statu quo* is mutual, but I leave him to apply it to his case according to his surroundings. I would not instruct him to undo all done by him between the actual date of our agreement and the time the knowledge reached him. I beg, therefore, to leave him free to apply the rule to his own case. Indeed, I have almost exceeded the bounds of prudence in checking him without the means of direct communication, and only did so on my absolute faith in your personal character.

I inclose a dispatch for General Wilson, in cipher, which, translated, simply advises him to keep his command well together, and to act according to the best of his ability, doing as little harm to the country as possible, until he knows hostilities are resumed.

I am, with respect,

W. T. SHERMAN,
Major-General U. S. A.

.

HEADQUARTERS MILITARY DIVISION OF THE MISSISSIPPI,
In the Field, Raleigh, N. C., April 23, 1865.

General WILSON :

⁂ Cipher dispatch received. There is a general suspension of hostilities, awaiting the assent of our new President to certain civil points before making a final military convention of peace. Act according to your own good sense until you are certain the war is over. Keep possession of some key-point that will secure your present advantages, rest your men and horses, and in a few days you will receive either positive information of peace, or may infer the contrary. My messenger should be back from Washington to-morrow.

W. T. SHERMAN, Major-General.

HEADQUARTERS MILITARY DIVISION OF THE MISSISSIPPI,
In the Field, Raleigh, N. C., April 23, 1865—8 P. M.

General JOSEPH E. JOHNSTON, *Confederate States Army* :

Major Hitchcock reports his arrival at Morehead City, with dispatches from Washington, and will be here in the morning. Please be ready to resume negotiations when the contents of dispatches are known.

Respectfully,

W. T. SHERMAN,

Major-General United States Army.

WAR DEPARTMENT,
Washington City, April 21, 1865.

GENERAL—The memorandum or basis agreed upon between General Sherman and General Johnston having been submitted to the President, they are disapproved. You will give notice of the disapproval to General Sherman, and direct him to resume hostilities at the earliest moment.

The instructions given to you by the late President, Abraham Lincoln, on the 3d of March, by my telegram of that date addressed to you, express substantially the views of President Andrew Johnson, and will be observed by General Sherman. A copy is herewith appended.

The President desires that you proceed immediately to the headquarters of General Sherman, and direct operations against the enemy.

Yours truly,

EDWIN M. STANTON, Secretary of War.

To Lieutenant-General GRANT.

COPY OF PRESIDENT LINCOLN'S INSTRUCTIONS.

WAR DEPARTMENT,
Washington City, March 3, 1865.

To Lieutenant-General GRANT :

The President directs me to say to you that he wishes you to have no conference with General Lee, unless it be for the capitulation of General Lee's army, or on some minor and purely military matter. He wishes me to say that you are not to decide, discuss, or confer upon any political question. Such questions the President holds in his own hands, and will submit them to no military conferences or conventions. Meantime you are to press to your utmost your military advantages.

EDWIN M. STANTON, Secretary of War.

HEADQUARTERS MILITARY DIVISION OF THE MISSISSIPPI,
In the Field, Raleigh, N. C., April 24, 1865—6 A. M.

General JOHNSTON, *Commanding Confederate Army, Greensboro'* :

You will take notice that the truce or suspension of hostilities agreed to between us will cease in forty-eight hours after this is received at your lines, under first of the articles of our agreement.

W. T. SHERMAN, Major-General.

HEADQUARTERS MILITARY DIVISION OF THE MISSISSIPPI,
In the Field, Raleigh, April 24, 1865.

General WILSON, *Macon* :

The truce will expire on the morning of the 26th. You will renew your operations according to your original instructions.

W. T. SHERMAN, Major-General commanding.

IN THE FIELD, Greensboro', April 24, 1865.

To Major-General W. T. SHERMAN, *Commanding :*

In forwarding the following dispatch, I respectfully suggest the propriety of releasing prisoners taken at Macon, and withdrawal of General Wilson's troops to some point beyond that at which he received from General Cobb information of the armistice.

J. E. JOHNSTON, General.

·————

HEADQUARTERS MILITARY DIVISION OF THE MISSISSIPPI,
In the Field, Raleigh, April 24, 1865.

General JOHNSTON, *Commanding Confederate Armies :*

I have replies from Washington to my communications of April 18. I am instructed to limit my operations to your immediate command, and not to attempt civil negotiations. I therefore demand the surrender of your army, on the same terms as were given to General Lee at Appomattox, of April 9, purely and simply.

W. T. SHERMAN, Major-General.

————

HEADQUARTERS ARMY OF THE TENNESSEE,
In the Field, April 25, 1865.

Major-General SHERMAN, *United States Army :*

Your dispatch of yesterday received. I propose a modification of the terms you offered ; such terms for the army as you wrote on the 18th ; they also modified according to change of circumstances, and a further armistice to arrange details and meeting for that purpose.

JOS. E. JOHNSTON, General.

Major-General W. T. SHERMAN, *Commanding United States Forces:*

GENERAL.—I have had the honor to receive your dispatch of yesterday, summoning this army to surrender on the terms accepted by General Lee at Appomattox Courthouse. I propose, instead of such surrender, terms based on those drawn up by you on the 18th for disbanding this army, and a further armistice and a conference to arrange these terms.

The disbanding of General Lee's army has afflicted this country with numerous bands having no means of subsistence but robbery. A knowledge of which would, I am sure, induce you to agree to other conditions.

Most respectfully, your obedient servant,

J. E. JOHNSTON, General.

HEADQUARTERS MILITARY DIVISION OF THE MISSISSIPPI,
In the Field, Raleigh, April 25, 1865.

GENERAL JOHNSTON—I will meet you at the same place as before, to-morrow, at 12 o'clock noon.

W. T. SHERMAN, Major-General.

[Telegram.]

GREENSBORO', April 26, 1865, 2 A. M.

Major-General SHERMAN, *through General* BUTLER:

I will meet you at time and place you designate. Is armistice with *status quo* renewed?

J. E. JOHNSTON, General.

TERMS OF THE CONVENTION.

Terms of a military convention entered into this twenty-sixth (26th) day of April, 1865, at Bennett's house, near Durham's Station, North Carolina, between General JOSEPH E. JOHNSTON, commanding the Confederate Army, and Major-General W. T. SHERMAN, commanding the United States Army in North Carolina.

ALL acts of war on the part of the troops under General Johnston's command to cease from this date. All arms and public property to be deposited at Greensboro', and delivered to an ordnance officer of the United States Army. Rolls of all the officers and men to be made in duplicate, one copy to be retained by the commander of the troops, and the other to be given to an officer to be designated by General Sherman. Each officer and man to give his individual obligation in writing not to take up arms against the Government of the United States until properly released from this obligation. The side-arms of officers and their private horses and baggage to be retained by them.

This being done, all the officers and men will be permitted to return to their homes, not to be disturbed by the United States authorities so long as they observe their obligations and the laws in force where they may reside.

W. T. SHERMAN, Major-General,
Com. U. S. Forces in North Carolina.

J. E. JOHNSTON, General,
Com. C. S. Forces in North Carolina.

Approved: U. S. GRANT, Lieutenant-General.

RALEIGH, N. C., April 26, 1865.

GENERAL SHERMAN'S ORDERS ON PEACE.

SPECIAL FIELD ORDER, No. 58.

HEADQUARTERS MILITARY DIVISION OF THE MISSISSIPPI,
In the Field, Raleigh, N. C., April 19, 1865.

The general commanding announces to the army a suspension of hostilities, and an agreement with General Johnston and high officials, which, when formally ratified, will make peace from the Potomac to the Rio Grande. Until the absolute peace is arranged, a line passing through Tyrrell's Mount, Chapel University, Durham's Station, and West Point, on the Neuse River, will separate the two armies. Each army commander will group his camps entirely with a view to comfort, health, and good police. All the details of military discipline must still be maintained, and the general hopes and believes that in a very few days it will be his good fortune to conduct you all to your homes. The fame of this army for courage, industry, and discipline is admitted all over the world. Then let each officer and man see that it is not stained by any act of vulgarity, rowdyism, and petty crime. The cavalry will patrol the front of the line. General Howard will take charge of the district from Raleigh, up to the cavalry, General Slocum to the left of Raleigh and General Schofield in Raleigh right and rear. Quartermasters and commissaries will keep their supplies up to a light load for

the wagons, and the railroad superintendent will arrange
a depot for the convenience of each separate army.

By order of

MAJOR-GENERAL W. T. SHERMAN.

L. M. DAYTON, A. A. G.

SPECIAL FIELD ORDERS, No. 65.

HEADQUARTERS MILITARY DIVISION OF THE MISSISSIPPI,
In the Field, Raleigh, N. C., April 27, 1865.

The general commanding announces a further suspension of hostilities, and a final agreement with General
Johnston, which terminates the war as to the armies under
his command and the country east of the Chattahoochie.

Copies of the terms of convention will be furnished
Major-Generals Schofield, Gillmore, and Wilson, who are
specially charged with the execution of its details in the
Department of North Carolina, Department of the South,
and at Macon and Western Georgia.

Captain Myers, ordnance department, United States
Army, is hereby designated to receive the arms, etc., at
Greensboro'. Any commanding officer of a post may receive the arms of any detachment, and see that they are
properly stored and accounted for.

General Schofield will procure at once the necessary
blanks, and supply the other army commanders, that
uniformity may prevail; and great care must be taken that
all the terms and stipulations on our part be fulfilled with
the most scrupulous fidelity, while those imposed on our
hitherto enemies will be received in a spirit becoming a
brave and generous army.

Army commanders may at once loan to the inhabitants

such of the captured mules, horses, wagons, and vehicles as can be spared from immediate use; and the commanding generals of armies may issue provisions, animals, or any public supplies that can be spared, to relieve present wants, and to encourage the inhabitants to renew their peaceful pursuits, and to restore the relations of friendship among our fellow-citizens and countrymen.

Foraging will forthwith cease, and when necessity or long marches compel the taking of forage, provisions, or any kind of private property, compensation will be made on the spot; or, when the disbursing officers are not provided with funds, vouchers will be given in proper form, payable at the nearest military depot.

By order of

MAJOR-GEN. W. T. SHERMAN.

L. M. DAYTON, Assistant Adjutant-General.

SPECIAL FIELD ORDERS, No. 66.

HEADQUARTERS MILITARY DIVISION OF THE MISSISSIPPI,
In the Field, Raleigh, N. C., April 27, 1865.

Hostilities having ceased, the following changes and dispositions of the troops in the field will be made with as little delay as practicable:

I. The Tenth and Twenty-third corps will remain in the Department of North Carolina, and Major-General J. M. Schofield will transfer back to Major-General Gillmore, commanding Department of the South, the two brigades formerly belonging to the division of brevet Major-General Grover, at Savannah. The Third division, cavalry corps, brevet Major-General J. Kilpatrick commanding, is hereby transferred to the. Department of North Carolina, and

General Kilpatrick will report in person to Major-General Schofield for orders.

II. The cavalry command of Major-Gen. George Stoneman will return to East Tennessee, and that of brevet Major-General J. H. Wilson will be conducted back to the Tennessee River, in the neighborhood of Decatur, Alabama.

III. Major-General Howard will conduct the Army of the Tennessee to Richmond, Va., following roads substantially by Lewisburg, Warrenton, Lawrenceville, and Petersburg, or to the right of that line. Major-General Slocum will conduct the Army of Georgia to Richmond by roads to the left of the one indicated for General Howard, viz., by Oxford, Boydton, and Nottoway Court-house. These armies will turn in at this point the contents of their ordnance trains, and use the wagons for extra forage and provisions. These columns will be conducted slowly and in the best of order, and aim to be at Richmond, ready to resume the march, by the middle of May.

IV. The chief-quartermaster and commissary of the military division, Generals Easton and Beckwith, after making proper dispositions of their departments here, will proceed to Richmond and make suitable preparations to receive those columns, and to provide them for the further journey.

By order of

MAJOR-GEN. W. T. SHERMAN.

L. M. DAYTON, Assistant Adjutant-General.

ADDRESS OF GENERAL JOHNSTON

TO THE PEOPLE OF THE SOUTHERN STATES.

[The subjoined "card" of the Confederate commander is of considerable interest, inasmuch as it points out the influences that prompted him to surrender, and states the number of troops he had at the time thereof under his control.]

[From the Charlotte (N. C.) Democrat.]

WE lay before our readers the following letter from Gen. Joseph E. Johnston, stating the causes which induced him to make terms of surrender with General Sherman. We believe General Johnston's conduct, and his refusal to continue the war after all hope of success was vain, is generally approved; but, if any one has a doubt on this point, the reasons set forth by General Johnston will clearly show that he acted correctly and wisely:

CHARLOTTE, N. C., May 6, 1865.

Having made a convention with Major-General Sherman to terminate hostilities in North and South Carolina, Georgia, and Florida, it seems to me proper to put before the people of those States the condition of military affairs which rendered that measure absolutely necessary.

On the 26th of April, the day of the convention, by the returns of three lieutenant-generals of the Army of Tennessee (that under my command), the number of infantry and artillery present and absent was 70,510; the total present 18,578; the effective total, or fighting force, 14,179. On the 7th of April, the date of the last return I can find, the effective total of the cavalry was 5,440. But between the 7th and 26th April it was greatly reduced by events in Virginia and apprehensions of surrender. In South Carolina we had Young's division of cavalry, less than one thousand, besides reserves and State troops—together much inferior to the Federal force in that State. In Florida, we were as weak. In Georgia, our inadequate force had been captured at Macon. In Lieutenant-General Taylor's department, there were no means of opposing the formidable army under General Canby, which had taken Mobile; nor the cavalry under General Wilson, which had captured every other place of importance west of Augusta. The latter had been stopped at Macon by the armistice, as we had been at Greensboro', but its distance from Augusta being less than half of ours, that place was in its power.

To carry on the war, therefore, we had to depend upon the Army of the Tennessee alone. The United States could have brought against it twelve or fifteen times its number in the armies of Generals Grant, Sherman, and Canby. With such odds against us, without the means of procuring ammunition or repairing arms, without money or credit to provide food, it was impossible to continue the war except as robbers. The consequence of prolonging the struggle would only have been the destruction or dispersion of our bravest men, and great suffering of women and children by the desolation and ruin inevitable from the marching of two hundred thousand men through the country.

Having failed in an attempt to obtain terms giving security to citizens as well as soldiers, I had to choose between wantonly bringing the evils of war upon those I had chosen to defend, and averting those calamities with the confession that hopes were dead, which every thinking Southern man had already lost. I therefore stipulated with General Sherman for the security of the brave and true men committed to me on terms which also terminated hostilities in all the country over which my command extended, and announced it to your Governors by telegraph as follows:

"The disaster in Virginia, the capture by the enemy of all our workshops for the preparation of ammunition and repairing of arms, the impossibility of recruiting our little army, opposed to more than ten times its number, or of supplying it, except by robbing our own citizens, destroyed all hope of successful war. I have therefore made a military convention with Major-General Sherman to terminate hostilities in North and South Carolina, Georgia, and Florida. I made this convention to spare the blood of this gallant little army, to prevent further suffering of our people by the devastation and ruin inevitable from the marches of invading armies, and to avoid the crime of waging a hopeless war."

J. E. JOHNSTON.

GENERAL SHERMAN'S EXAMINATION

BEFORE THE CONGRESSIONAL COMMITTEE ON THE CONDUCT OF THE
WAR, RELATIVE TO HIS CONFERENCE WITH GENERAL JOSEPH E.
JOHNSTON.

MAJOR-GENERAL SHERMAN being sworn and examined :
By the Chairman—

Q. What is your rank in the army ? A. I am major-general in the regular army.

Q. As your negotiation with the rebel General Johnston, in relation to his surrender, has been the subject of much public comment, the committee desire you to state all the facts and circumstances in regard to it, or which you wish the public to know. A. On the 15th day of April last I was at Raleigh, in command of three armies, the Army of the Ohio, the Army of the Cumberland, and the Army of the Tennessee ; my enemy was General Joseph E. Johnston, of the Confederate army, who commanded fifty thousand men, retreating along the railroad from Raleigh, by Hillsboro', Greensboro', Salisbury, and Charlotte. I commenced pursuit by crossing the curve of that road in the direction of Ashboro' and Charlotte. After the head of my column had crossed the Cape Fear River at Aven's Ferry, I received a communication from General Johnston, and answered it, copies of which I most promptly sent to the War Department, with a letter addressed to the secretary of war, as follows :

HEADQUARTERS MILITARY DIVISION OF THE MISSISSIPPI,
In the Field, Raleigh, N. C., April 15.

General U. S. GRANT *and Secretary of War :*

I send copies of a correspondence to you with General Johnston, which I think will be followed by terms of capitulation. I will grant the same terms General Grant gave General Lee, and be careful not to complicate any points of civil policy. If any cavalry has retreated towards me, caution them to be prepared to find our work done. It is now raining in torrents, and I shall await General Johnston's reply here, and will prepare to meet him in person at Chapel Hill.

I have invited Governor Vance to return to Raleigh with the civil officers of his State. I have met ex-Governor Graham, Messrs. Badger, Moore, Holden, and others, all of whom agree that the war is over, and that the States of the South must resume their allegiance, subject to the Constitution and laws of Congress, and must submit to the national arms. This great fact was admitted, and the details are of easy arrangement.

W. T SHERMAN, Major-General.

I met General Johnston, in person, at a house five miles from Durham's Station, under a flag of truce. After a few preliminary remarks he said to me, since Lee had surrendered his army at Appomattox Court-house, of which he had just been advised, he looked upon further opposition by him as the greatest possible of crimes; that he wanted to know whether I could make him any general concessions; any thing by which he could maintain his hold and control of his army, and prevent its scattering; any thing to satisfy the great yearning of their people. If so, he thought he could arrange terms satisfactory to both parties. He wanted to embrace the condition and fate of all the armies of the Southern Confederacy to the Rio Grande, to make one job of it, as he termed it.

I asked him what his powers were,—whether he could

command and control the fate of all the armies to the Rio Grande. He answered that he thought he could obtain the power, but he did not possess it that moment; he did not know where Mr. Davis was, but he thought if I could give him the time, he could find Mr. Breckinridge, whose orders would be obeyed everywhere, and he could pledge me his personal faith that whatever he undertook to do would be done.

I had had frequent correspondence with the late President of the United States, with the secretary of war, with General Halleck, and with General Grant, and the general impression left upon my mind was, that if a settlement could be made, consistent with the Constitution of the United States, the laws of Congress, and the proclamation of the President, they would not only be willing, but pleased to terminate the war by one single stroke of the pen.

I needed time to finish the railroad from the Neuse Bridge up to Raleigh, and thought I could put in four or five days of good time in making repairs to my road, even if I had to send propositions to Washington. I therefore consented to delay twenty-four hours, to enable General Johnston to procure what would satisfy me as to his authority and ability, as a military man, to do what he undertook to do. I therefore consented to meet him the next day, the 17th, at 12 o'clock noon, at the same place.

We did meet again; after a general interchange of courtesies, he remarked that he was then prepared to satisfy me that he could fulfil the terms of our conversation of the day before. He then asked me what I was willing to do. I told him, in the first place, I could not deal with anybody except men recognized by us as "belligerents," because no military man could go beyond that fact. The attorney-general has since so decided, and any man of common sense so understood it before; there was no difference upon that point as to the men and officers accompanying the Confederate armies. I told him that the President of the United States, by a published proclamation, had enabled every man in the Southern Confederate army, of the rank of colonel and under, to procure and obtain amnesty, by simply taking the oath of allegiance to the United States, and agreeing to go to his home and live in peace. The terms of General Grant to General Lee extended the same principles to the officers, of the rank of brigadier-general and upward, including the highest officer in the Confederate army, viz., General Lee, the commander-in-chief. I was, therefore, willing to proceed with him upon the same principles.

Then a conversation arose as to what form of government they were to have in the South. Were the States there to be dissevered, and were the people to be denied representation in Congress? Were the people there to be, in the common language of the people of the South, slaves to the people of the North? Of course, I said "No; we desire that you shall regain your position as citizens of the United States, free and equal to us in all respects, and wish representation upon the condition of submission to the lawful authority of the United States as defined by the Constitution, the United States courts, and the authorities of the United States supported by those courts." He then remarked to me that General Breckinridge, a major-general in the Confederate army, was near by, and if I had no objection he would like to have him present. I called his attention to the fact that I had, on the day before, explained to him that any negotiations between us must be confined to belligerents. He replied that he understood that perfectly. " But," said he, " Breckinridge, whom you do not know, save by public rumor as secretary of war, is, in fact, a major-general; I give you my word for that. Have you any objection to his being present as a major-general?" I replied, " I have no objection to any military officer you desire being present as a part of your personal staff." I, myself, had my own officers near me at call.

Breckinridge came, a stranger to me, whom I had never spoken to in my life, and he joined in the conversation; while that conversation was going on a courier arrived and handed to General Johnston a package of papers; he and Breckinridge sat down and looked over them for some time, and put them away in their pockets: what they were, I knew not, but one of them was a slip of paper, written, as General Johnston told me, by Mr. Reagan, postmaster-general of the Southern Confederacy: they seemed to talk about it *sotto voce,* and finally handed it to me; I glanced over it; it was preceded by a preamble and closed with a few general terms: I rejected it at once.

We then discussed matters; talked about slavery, talked about every thing. There was a universal assent that slavery was as dead as any thing could be; that it was one of the issues of the war long since determined; and even General Johnston laughed at the folly of the Confederate government in raising negro soldiers, whereby they gave us all the points of the case. I told them that slavery had been treated by us as a dead institution, first by one class of men from the initiation of the war, and then from the date of the Emancipation Proclamation of President Lincoln, and finally by the assent of all parties. As to reconstruction, I told them I did not know what the views of the administration were. Mr. Lincoln, up to that time, in letters and by telegrams to me, encouraged me by all the words which could be used in general terms, to believe, not only in his willingness, but in his desires that I should make terms with civil authorities, governors, and legislatures, even as far back as 1863. It then occurred to me that I might write off some general propositions, meaning little or meaning much, according to the construction of parties—what I would term "glittering generalities"—and send them to Washington, which I could do in four days. That would enable the new President to give me a clue to his policy in the important juncture which was then upon us, for the war was over; the highest military authorities of the Southern Confederacy so confessed to me openly, unconcealedly, and repeatedly. I therefore drew up the memorandum (which has been published to the world)* for the purpose of referring it to the proper executive authority of the United States, and enabling him to define to me what I might promise, simply to cover the pride of the Southern men, who thereby became subordinate to the laws of the United States, civil and military. I made no concessions to General Johnston's army, or the troops under his direction and immediate control; and if any concessions were made in those general terms, they were made because I then believed, and now believe, they would have delivered into the hands of the United States the absolute control of every Confederate officer and soldier, all their muster-rolls, and all their arms. It would save us all the incidental expense resulting from the military occupation of that country by provost-marshals, provost-guards, military governors, and all the machinery by which alone military power can reach the people of a civilized country. It would have surrendered to us the armies of Dick Tay-

---

* Printed in the last chapter of this volume.

lor and Kirby Smith, both of them capable of doing infinite mischief to us, by exhausting the resources of the whole country upon which we were to depend for the future extinguishment of our debt, forced upon us by their wrongful and rebellious conduct. I never designed to shelter a human being from any liability incurred in consequence of past acts to the civil tribunals of our country, and I do not believe a fair and manly interpretation of my terms can so construe them, for the words "United States courts," "United States authorities," "limitations of executive power," occur in every paragraph. And if they seemingly yield terms better than the public would desire to be given to the Southern people, if studied closely and well it will be found that there is an absolute submission on their part to the Government of the United States, either through its executive, legislative, or judicial authorities. Every step in the programme of these negotiations was reported punctually, clearly, and fully, by the most rapid means of communication that I had. And yet I neglected not one single precaution necessary to reap the full benefits of my position, in case the Government amended, altered, or absolutely annulled those terms. As those matters were necessarily mingled with the military history of the period, I would like, at this point, to submit to the committee my official report, which has been in the hands of the proper officer, Brigadier-General Rawlings, chief of staff of the Army of the United States, since about the 12th inst. It was made by me at Manchester, Va., after I had returned from Savannah, whither I went to open up the Savannah River, and reap the fruits of my negotiations with General Johnston, and to give General Wilson's force in the interior a safe and sure base from which he could draw the necessary supply of clothing and food for his command. It was only after I fulfilled all this that I learned for the first time, through the public press, that my conduct had been animadverted upon, not only by the secretary of war, but by General Halleck and the press of the country at large.* I did feel hurt and annoyed that Mr. Stanton coupled with the terms of my memorandum, confided to him, a copy of a telegram to General Grant, which he had never sent to me. He knew, on the contrary, that when he was at Savannah, I had negotiations with civil parties there, for he was present in my room when those parties were conferring with me; and I wrote him a letter, setting forth many points of it, in which I said I aimed to make a split in Jeff. Davis's dominions, by segregating Georgia from their course. Those were civil negotiations, and, far from being discouraged from making them, I was encouraged by Secretary Stanton himself to make them.

By coupling the note to General Grant with my memorandum, he gave the world fairly and clearly to infer that I was in possession of it. Now I was not in possession of it, and I have reason to know that Mr. Stanton knew I was not in possession of it. Next met me General Halleck's telegram, indorsed by Mr. Stanton, in which they publicly avowed an act of perfidy—namely, the violation of my terms, which I had a right to make, and which, by the laws of war and by the laws of Congress, is punishable by death, and no other punishment.* Next, they ordered an army to pursue my enemy, who was known to be surrendering to me, in the presence of General Grant himself, their superior officer; and, finally, they sent orders to Gen-

---

* Secretary Stanton's and General Halleck's "animadversions" are given in the concluding chapter.

eral Wilson and to General Thomas—my subordinates, acting under me on a plan of the most magnificent scale, admirably executed—to defeat my orders, and to thwart the interests of the Government of the United States. I did feel indignant—I do feel indignant. As to my own honor, I can protect it. In my letter of the 15th of April I used this language: "I have invited Governor Vance to return to Raleigh, with the civil officers of his State." I did so because President Lincoln had himself encouraged me to a similar course with the governor of Georgia, when I was in Atlanta. And here was the opportunity which the secretary of war should have taken to put me on my guard against making terms with civil authorities, if such were the settled policy of our Government. Had President Lincoln lived, I know he would have sustained me.

The following is my report, which I desire to have incorporated into, and made part of, my testimony:

[General Sherman here introduced his official Report, dated, " City Point, Va., May 9," which forms Part IV. of this work.]

Q. Did you have, near Fortress Monroe, a conference with President Lincoln; and if so, about what time? A. I met General Grant and Mr. Lincoln on board a steamboat, lying at the wharf at City Point, during the evening of the 27th of March; I resumed my visit to the President on board the same steamer anchored in the stream the following day, General Grant being present on both occasions.

Q. In those conferences was any arrangement made with you and General Grant, or either of you, in regard to the manner of arranging business with the Confederacy in regard to terms of peace? A. Nothing definite; it was simply a matter of general conversation, nothing specific and definite.

Q. At what time did you learn that President Lincoln had assented to the assembling of the Virginia rebel Legislature ?   A. I knew of it on the 18th of April, I think, but I procured a paper with the specific order of General Weitzel, also a copy of the amnesty proclamation on the 20th of April.

Q. You did not know, at that time, that that arrangement had been rescinded by the President ?   A. No, sir; I did not know that until afterwards; the moment I heard of that I notified General Johnston of it.

Q. Then at the time you entered into this arrangement with General Johnston, you knew that General Weitzel had approved of the calling together of the rebel Legislature of Virginia, by the assent of the President ?   A. I knew of it by some source unofficially; I succeeded in getting a copy of the paper containing General Weitzel's order on the 20th or 21st of April.*

Q. But at the time of your arrangement you did not know that that order had been rescinded ?   A. No, sir; I learned that several days afterwards, and at once sent word to General Johnston.

Q. At the time of your arrangement you also knew of the surrender of Lee's army, and the terms of that surrender ?   A. I had that officially from General Grant; I got that at Smithfield, on the 12th of April.

Q. I have what purports to be a letter from you to Johnston, which seems to imply that you intended to make the arrangement on the terms of Lee's surrender. The letter is as follows :

---

* The "call" for the Virginia Legislature is given at the end of this work.

HEADQUARTERS MILITARY DIVISION OF THE MISSISSIPPI,
In the Field, Raleigh, N. C., April 14.

General J. E. JOHNSTON, *Commanding Confederate Army :*

GENERAL.—I have this moment received your communication of this date. I am fully empowered to arrange with you any time for the suspension of further hostilities as between the armies commanded by myself and you, and will be willing to confer with you to that end. I will limit the advance of my main column to-morrow to Morristown, and the cavalry to the University, and I expect you will maintain the present position of your forces until each has notice of a failure to agree.

That a basis of action may be had, I undertake to abide by the same terms and conditions as were made by Generals Grant and Lee at Appomattox Court-house, on the 9th instant, relative to the two armies; and furthermore, to obtain from General Grant an order to suspend the movements of any troops from the direction of Virginia. General Stoneman is under my command, and my orders will suspend any devastation or destruction contemplated by him. I will add that I really desire to save the people of North Carolina the damage they would sustain by the march of this army through the central or western parts of the State.

I am, with respect, your obedient servant,

W. T. SHERMAN, Major-General.

A. Those were the terms as to his own army; but the concessions I made him were for the purpose of embracing other armies.

Q. And the writings you signed were to include other armies? A. The armies of Kirby Smith and Dick Taylor, so that afterwards no man within the limits of the Southern Confederacy could claim to belong to any Confederate army in existence.

Q. The President addressed a note to General Grant, perhaps not to you, to the effect of forbidding officers of the army from entering into any thing but strictly military arrangements, leaving civil matters entirely to him? A. I never saw such a note signed by President Lincoln; Mr. Stanton made such a note or telegram, and says it was by President Lincoln's dictation; he made it to General Grant, but never to me; on the contrary, while I was in Georgia, Mr. Lincoln telegraphed to me encouraging me to discuss matters with Governor Brown and Mr. Stephens.

Q. Then you had no notice of that order to General Grant? A. I had no knowledge of it, officially or otherwise.

Q. In the published report of your agreement there is nothing about slavery, I believe? A. There was nothing said about slavery, because it did not fall within the category of military questions, and we could not make it so. It was a legal question which the President had disposed of, overriding all our action. We had to treat the slave as *free*, because the President, our commander-in-chief, said he was free. For me to have renewed the question when that decision was made, would have involved the absurdity of an inferior undertaking to qualify the work of his superior.

Q. That was the reason why it was not mentioned? A. Yes, sir; subsequently I wrote a note to Johnston, stating that I thought it would be well to mention it for political effect, when we came to draw up the final terms with precision: that note was written pending the time my memorandum was going to Washington, and before an answer had been returned.

Q. At the time you entered into these negotiations was Johnston in a condition to offer any effective resistance to your army? A. He could not have resisted my army an hour, if I could have got hold of him; but he could have escaped from me by breaking up into small parties, or by taking the country roads, travelling faster than my army, with trains, could have pursued.

Q. Then your object in negotiating was to keep his army from scattering into guerrilla bands? A. That was my chief object; I so officially notified the War Department.

Q. And not because there was any doubt about the result of a battle? A. There was no question as to the result of a battle, and I knew it; every soldier knew it. Johnston said, in the first five minutes of our conversation, that any further resistance on his part would be an act of folly, and all he wanted was to keep his army from dispersing.

By Mr. Loan—

Q. In your examination by the chairman you stated that you were acting in pursuance of instructions from Mr. Lincoln, derived from his letters and telegrams at different times? A. Yes, sir.

Q. Have you any of these letters and telegrams which you can furnish to the committee? A. I can furnish you a copy of a dispatch to General Halleck from Atlanta, in which I stated that I had invited Governor Brown and Vice-President Stevens to meet us; and I can give you a copy of Mr. Lincoln's answer, for my dispatch was referred to him, in which he said he felt much interested in my dispatch, and encouraged me to allow their visit: but the letter to which I referred specifically was a longer letter which I wrote to General Halleck from my camp on Big Black, Mississippi, at General Halleck's instigation, in September, 1863, which was received in Washington, and submitted to Mr. Lincoln, who desired to have it published, to which I would not consent; in that letter I gave my opinions fully and frankly, not only upon the military situation, but also the civil policy necessary; Mr. Lincoln expressed himself highly pleased with my views, and desired to make them public, but I preferred not to do so.

Q. And by subsequent acts he induced you to believe he approved of these views? A. I *know* he approved of them, and always encouraged me to carry out those views.

By the Chairman—

Q. The following is a letter published in the newspapers, purporting to have been addressed by you to Johnston, dated April 21, 1865 :.

HEADQUARTERS, MILITARY DIVISION OF THE MISSISSIPPI,
In the Field, Raleigh, N. C., April 21.

General J. E. JOHNSTON, *Commanding Confederate Army :*

GENERAL—I send you a letter for General Wilson, which, if sent by telegraph and courier, will check his career. He may mistrust the telegraph ; therefore better send the original, for he cannot mistake my handwriting, with which he is familiar. He seems to have his blood up, and will be hard to hold. If he can buy corn, fodder, and rations down about Fort Valley it will obviate the necessity of his going up to Rome or Dalton.

It is reported to me from Cairo that Mobile is in our possession, but it is not minute or official.

General Baker sent in to me, wanting to surrender his command, on the theory that the whole Confederate army was surrendered. I explained to him, or his staff officer, the exact truth, and left him to act as he thought proper. He seems to have disbanded his men, deposited a few arms about twenty miles from here, and himself awaits your action. I will not hold him, his men, or arms, subject to any condition other than the final one we may agree upon.

I shall look for Major Hitchcock back from Washington on Wednesday, and shall promptly notify you of the result. By the action of General Weitzel in relation to the Virginia Legislature, I feel certain we will have no trouble on the score of recognizing existing State governments. It may be the lawyers will want us to define more minutely what is meant by the guarantee of rights of persons and property. It may be construed into a compact for us to undo the past as to the rights of slaves and leases of plantations on the Mississippi of vacant and abandoned plantations. I wish you would talk to the best men you have on these points; and if possible, let us, in our final convention, make these points so clear as to leave no room for angry controversy. I believe if the South would simply and publicly declare what we feel, that slavery is dead, that you would inaugurate an era of peace and prosperity that would soon efface the ravages of the past four years of war. Negroes would remain in the South, and afford you abundance of cheap labor, which otherwise will be driven away; and it will save the country the senseless discussions which have kept us all in hot water for fifty years.

Although, strictly, this is no subject for a military convention, yet I am honestly convinced that our simple declarations of a result will be accepted as good law everywhere. Of course, I have not a single word from Washington on this or any other point of our agreement, but I know the effect of such a step by us will be universally accepted.

> I am, with great respect,
> Your obedient servant,
> W. T. SHERMAN, Major-Gen. U. S. A.

Q. This is the letter in which you say that it would be well to declare publicly that slavery is dead? A. Yes, sir; that is the letter.

By Mr. Loan—

Q. Will you furnish the committee a copy of the letter written by you to Mr. Stanton, in January last, from Savannah? A. I will do so.

*Mr. Chairman—*And when the manuscript of your testimony is prepared it will be remitted to you for revision, and you can add to it any statement or papers that you may subsequently desire or consider necessary.

I have the above, and now subjoin copies of letters from my letter-book, in the order of the bringing in the questions revised by this inquiry:

HEADQUARTERS MIDDLE DEPARTMENT OF THE MISSISSIPPI,
In the Field, Raleigh, N. C., April 18, 1865.

To Lieutenant-General U. S. GRANT, *or Major-General* HALLECK,
Washington, D. C. :

GENERAL.—I inclose herewith a copy of an agreement made this day between General Joseph E. Johnston and myself, which, if approved by the President of the United States, will produce peace from the Potomac to the Rio Grande. Mr. Breckinridge was present at the conference in the capacity of major-general, and satisfied me of the ability of General Johnston to carry out to the full extent the terms of this agreement ; and if you will get the President to simply indorse the copy, and commission me to carry out the terms, I will follow them to the conclusion. You will observe that it is an absolute submission of the enemy to the lawful authorities of the United States, and disperses his armies absolutely ; and the point to which I attach most importance is, that the disposition and dispersement of the armies is done in such a manner as to prevent them breaking up into a guerrilla crew. On the other hand, we can retain just as much of an army as we please. I agree to the mode and manner of the surrender of armies set forth, as it gives the States the means of suppressing guerrillas, which we could not expect them to do if we strip them of all arms.

Both Generals Johnston and Breckinridge admitted that slavery was dead, and I could not insist on embracing it in such a paper, because it can be made with the States in detail. I knew that all the men of substance South sincerely want peace, and I do not believe they will resort to war again during this century. I have no doubt but that they will in the future be perfectly subordinate to the laws of the United States. The moment my action in this matter is approved, I can spare five corps, and will ask for and have General Schofield here with the Tenth Corps, and go myself with the Fourteenth, Fifteenth, Seventeenth, Twentieth, and Twenty-third corps, *via* Burkesville and Gordonsville, to Frederick or Hagerstown, there to be paid and mustered out.

The question of finance is now the chief one, and every soldier and officer not needed ought to go home at once. I would like to be able to begin the march North by May 1.

I urge on the part of the President speedy action, as it is important to get the Confederate armies to their homes, as well as our own.

I am, with great respect, your obedient servant,

W. T. SHERMAN, Major-General commanding.

HEADQUARTERS MIDDLE DEPARTMENT OF THE MISSISSIPPI,
In the Field, Raleigh, N. C., April 18.

General H. W. HALLECK, Chief of Staff, Washington, D. C. :

GENERAL—I received your dispatch describing the man Clark, detailed to assassinate me. He had better be in a hurry, or he will be too late. The news of Mr. Lincoln's death produced almost intense effect on our troops. At first I feared it would lead to excesses, but now it has softened down, and can easily be quieted. None evince more feeling than General Johnston, who admitted that the act was calculated to stain his cause with a dark hue ; and he contended that the loss was most severe on the South, who had begun to realize that Mr. Lincoln was the best friend the South had.

I cannot believe that even Mr. Davis was privy to the diabolical plot, but think it the emanation of a lot of young men of the South, who are very devils. I want to throw upon the South the care of this class of men, who will soon be as obnoxious to their industrious class as to us.

Had I pushed Johnston's army to an extremity, it would have dispersed and done infinite mischief. Johnston informed me that General Stoneman had been at Salisbury, and was now about Statesville. I have sent him orders to come to me.

General Johnston also informed me that General Wilson was at Columbus, Ga., and he wanted me to arrest his progress. I leave that to you. Indeed, if the President sanctions my agreement with Johnston, our interest is to cease all destruction. Please give all orders necessary, according to the views the executive may take, and inform him, if possible, not to vary the terms at all, for I have considered every thing, and believe that the Confederate armies are dispersed. We can adjust all else fairly and well.

I am yours, etc.,

W. T. SHERMAN, Major-General commanding.

Lest confusion should result to the mind of the committee by the latter part of the above letter, I state it was addressed to General Halleck, as chief of staff, when he was in the proper " line of order" to the commander-in-chief. The whole case changed when, on the 26th of April, he became the commander of the separate division of the James.

As stated in my testimony, General Grant reached Raleigh on the 24th, and on the 25th, on the supposition that I would start next day to chase Johnston's army, I wrote him the following letter, delivered in person :

HEADQUARTERS DEPARTMENT OF THE MISSISSIPPI,
In the Field, Raleigh, N. C., April 25.

Lieutenant-General U. S. GRANT—*Present :*

GENERAL—I received your letter of April 21, with inclosures, yesterday, and was well pleased that you came along, as you must have observed that I held the military control, so as to adapt it to any phase the case might assume.

It is but just that I should record the fact that I made my terms with General Johnston under the influence of the liberal terms you extended to the army of General Lee, at Appomattox Court-house, on the 9th ; and the seeming policy of our Government, as evinced by the call of the Virginia Legislature and governor back to Richmond, under yours and President Lincoln's very eyes. It now appears this last act was done without any consultation with you, or any knowledge of Mr. Lincoln, but rather in opposition to a previous policy well considered.

I have not the least desire to interfere in the civil policy of our Government, but would shun it as something not to my liking. But occasions arise when a prompt seizure of results is forced on military commanders not in immediate communication with the proper authority. It is possible that the terms signed by General Johnston and myself were not clear enough on the point well understood between us—that our negotiations did not apply to any parties outside the officers and men of the Confederate armies, which could easily have been remedied.

No surrender of any army, not actually at the mercy of the antagonist, was ever made without "terms," and those always define the military status of the surrendered. Thus you stipulated that the officers and men of Lee's army should not be molested at their homes, so long as they obeyed the laws at the place of their residence. I do not wish to discuss these points, involved in our recognition of the State governments in actual existence, but will merely state my conclusion, to await the solution of the future.

Such action, on one point, in no manner recognizes for a moment the so-called Confederate government, or makes us liable for its debts or acts. The laws and acts done by the several States, during the period of rebellion, are *void*, because done without the oath prescribed by the Constitution of the United States, which is a condition precedent. We have a right to use any sort of machinery to produce military results; and it is the commonest thing for military commanders to use the civil government, *in actual existence*, as a means to an end. I do believe we could and can use the present State governments lawfully, constitutionally, and as the very best possible means to produce the object desired, viz., entire and complete submission to the lawful authority of the United States.

As to punishment of past crimes, that is for the judiciary, and can in no manner or way be disturbed by our acts; and, so far as I can, I will use my influence that rebels shall suffer all the personal punishment provided by law, as also the civil liabilities accruing from this past act.

What we now want, is the new form of law by which common men may regain their position of industry, so long disturbed by the war.

I now apprehend that the rebel army will disperse, and instead of dealing with six or seven States, we will have to deal with numberless bands of desperadoes, headed by such men as Moseby, Forrest, Red Jackson, and others, who know not and care not for danger and its consequences.

I am, with great respect, your obedient servant,

W. T. SHERMAN, Major-General.

On the same day I wrote and mailed to the secretary of war the following:

HEADQUARTERS MIDDLE DIVISION OF THE MISSISSIPPI,
In the Field, Raleigh, N. C. April 25.

Hon. E. M. STANTON, Secretary of War, Washington:

DEAR SIR—I have been furnished a copy of your letter of April 21st, to General Grant, signifying your disapproval of the terms on which General Johnston proposed to disarm and disperse the insurgents, on condition of amnesty, etc. I admit my folly in embracing, in a military convention, any civil matter ; but, unfortunately, such is the nature of our situation, that they seem inextricably united, and I understood from you at Savannah that the financial state of the country demanded military success, and would warrant a little lending to policy.

When I had my conference with General Johnston, I had the public example before me of General Grant's terms to Lee's army, and General Weitzel's invitation to the Virginia Legislature to assemble. I still believe that General Grant, of the United States army, has made a mistake ; but that is none of my business. Mine is a different task ; and I had flattered myself that by four years of patient and unremitting and successful labor, I deserved no reminder such as is contained in the last paragraph of your letter to General Grant.

You may assure the President that I need his suggestion.

I am, truly, etc.,

W. T. SHERMAN, Major-General commanding.

The last sentence refers to the fact that General Grant had been sent to Raleigh to direct military movements. That was the first time in my life I had ever had a word of reproof from the Government of the United States, and I was naturally sensitive. But all I said to any one was to General Meigs, who came with General Grant: "It was not kind on the part of Mr. Secretary Stanton." The fact known did not gratify any military conduct. The first interview with General Johnston followed, and the terms of capitulation were agreed upon and signed, and General Grant started for Washington bearing the news.

When, on the 28th of April, I received, in the New York *Times*, the most extraordinary budget of Mr. Stanton, which for the first time startled me, I wrote to General Grant this letter

HEADQUARTERS MILITARY DIVISION OF THE MISSISSIPPI,
In the Field, April 28.

Lieutenant-General U. S. GRANT, *General-in-Chief, Washington, D. C.:*

GENERAL—Since you left me yesterday, I have seen the New York *Times* of the 24th inst., containing a budget of military news, authenticated by the signature of the secretary of war, which is grouped in such a way as to give very erroneous impressions. It embraces a copy of the basis of agreement between myself and General Johnston, of April 18th, with commentaries, which it will be time enough to discuss two or three years hence, after the Government has experimented a little more in the machinery by which power reaches the scattered people of the vast country known as the South. But in the mean time, I do think that my rank (if not past services) entitle me, at least, to the respect of keeping secret what was known to none but the cabinet, until further inquiry comes to be made, instead of giving publicity to documents I never saw, and drawing inferences wide of the truth.

I never saw, or had furnished me, a copy of Mr. Stanton's dispatch to you of the 3d of March, nor did Mr. Stanton, or any human being, ever convey to me its substance, or any thing like it; but, on the contrary, I had seen General Weitzel's, in relation to the Virginia Legislature, made in Mr. Lincoln's very person, and had failed to discover any other official hints of the plan of reconstruction, or any idea calculated to allay the fears of the people of the South, after the destruction of their armies and civil authorities would leave them without any government at all.

We should not drive a people to anarchy, and it is simply impossible for one military power to waste all the masses of this unhappy country.

I confess I did not want to drive General Johnston's army into the hands of armed men, going about without purpose, and capable only of indefinite mischief.

But you saw, on your arrival at Raleigh, that I had my armies so disposed, that his escape was only possible in a disorganized shape; and, as you did not choose to direct military operations in this quarter, I infer that you were satisfied with the military situation.

At all events, the moment I learned, what was proper enough, the disapproval of the President, I wished in such manner to compel the surrender of Johnston's whole army on the same terms as you had prescribed to General Lee's army, when you had it surrounded, and in your absolute power.

Mr. Stanton, in stating that my order to General Stoneman was likely to result in the escape of "Mr. Davis to Mexico or Europe," is in deep error.

General Stoneman was not at Salisbury then, but had gone back to Statesville. Davis was supposed to be between us, and Stoneman was beyond him.

By turning towards me he was approaching Davis; and, had he joined me as I ordered, I then would have had a mounted force needed for that and other purposes. But even now I don't know that Mr. Stanton wants Davis caught. And as my official papers, deemed sacred, are hastily published to the world, it will be imprudent for me to state what has been done in this respect.

As the editor of the *Times* has (it may be) logically and fairly drawn the inference from this singular document, that I am insubordinate, I can only deny the intention.* I have never in my life questioned or disobeyed an order, though many and many a time I have risked my life, my health, and reputation in obeying orders, or even hints, to execute plans and purposes not to my liking. It is not fair to withhold from me plans and policy (if any there be), and expect me to guess at them; for facts and events appear quite different from different stand-points. For four years I have been in camp, dealing with soldiers, and I can assure you that the conclusion at which the cabinet arrived with such singular unanimity differs from mine. I have conferred freely with the best officers in this army as to the points involved in this controversy, and, strange to say, they were singularly unanimous in the other conclusion, and they will learn with pain and sorrow that I am deemed insubordinate, and

---

* The editorial of the New York *Times*, here referred to, is given in the concluding chapter.

wanting in common sense; that I, who have labored day and night, winter and summer, for four years, and have brought an army of seventy thousand men in magnificent condition across a country deemed impassable, and placed it just where it was wanted almost on the day appointed, have brought discredit on the Government.

I do not wish to boast of this, but I do say that it entitled me to the courtesy of being consulted before publishing to the world a proposition rightfully submitted to higher authority for adjudication, and then accompanied by statements which invited the press to be let loose on me.

It is true that non-combatants—men who sleep in comfort and security, while we watch on the distant lines—are better able to judge than we poor soldiers, who rarely see a newspaper, hardly can hear from our families, or stop long enough to get our pay. I envy not the task of reconstruction, and am delighted that the secretary has relieved me of it.

As you did not undertake to assume the management of the affairs of this army, I infer that, on personal inspection, your mind arrived at a different conclusion from that of Mr. Secretary Stanton. I will therefore go on and execute your orders to the conclusion, and when done, will, with intense satisfaction, leave to the civil authorities the execution of the task of which they seem to me so jealous; but, as an honest man and soldier, I invite them to follow my path, for they may see some things and hear some things that may disturb their philosophy.

With sincere respect,

W. T. SHERMAN, Major-General commanding.

P. S.—As Mr. Stanton's singular paper has been published, I demand that this also be made public, though I am in no way responsible to the press, but to the law and my proper superiors.

W. T. SHERMAN, Major-Gen. commanding.

Since my arrival at Washington, I have learned from General Grant that this letter was received, but he preferred to withhold it until my arrival, as he knew I was making towards Washington with my army. Upon my arrival, I did not insist on its publication till it was drawn out by this inquiry. I also append here the copy of a letter from Colonel T. S. Bowers, A. A. G., asking me to modify my reports as to the point of violating my truce, with my answer.

HEADQUARTERS ARMIES OF THE UNITED STATES,
Washington, May 25.

Major-General W. T. SHERMAN, *Commanding Military Division of the Mississippi :*

General Grant directed me to call your attention to the part of your report in which the necessity of maintaining your truce at the expense of many lives, is spoken of. The general thinks that in making a truce the commander of an army can control only his own army, and that the hostile general must make his own arrangements with other armies acting against him.

While independent generals acting against a common foe would naturally act in concert, the general claims that each must be the judge of his own duty and responsible for its execution.

If you should wish, the report will be returned for any change you may deem best.

Very respectfully,
Your obedient servant,
T. S. BOWERS,
Assistant Adjutant-General.

HEADQUARTERS MILITARY DIVISION OF THE MISSISSIPPI,
Washington, D. C., May 26.

Colonel T. S. BOWERS, *Assistant Adjutant-General, Washington, D. C. :*

COLONEL—I had the honor to receive your letter of May 25, last evening, and I hasten to answer. I wish to precede it by renewing the assurance of my entire confidence and respect for the President and Lieutenant-General Grant, and that in all matters I will be most willing to shape my official and private conduct to suit their wishes. The past is beyond my control, and the matters embraced in the official report to which you refer are finished. It is but just the reasons that actuated me, right or wrong, should stand on record ; but in all future cases, should any arise, I will respect the decisions of General Grant, though I think them wrong.

Suppose a guard has prisoners in charge, and officers of another command should aim to rescue or kill them, is it not clear the guard must defend the prisoners as a safeguard ? So jealous is the military law to protect and maintain *good faith* when pledged, that the law adjudges death, and no alternative punishment, to one who violates a safeguard in foreign ports. (See Articles of War, No. 55.) For murder, arson, treason, and the highest military crimes, the punishment prescribed by law is death, or some minor punishment ; but for the violation of a " safeguard," death, and death alone, is the prescribed penalty. I instance this to illustrate how, in military stipulations to an enemy, our Government commands and enforces " good faith." In discussing this matter I would like to refer to many writers on military law, but am willing to take Halleck as the text. (See his chapter, No. 27.)

In the very first article he states that *good faith* should always be observed between enemies in war, because when our faith has been pledged to him, so far as the promise extends, he ceases to be an enemy. He then defines the meaning of *compacts* and *conventions*, and says they are made sometimes for a general or a partial suspension of hostilities for the " surrender of an army," etc. They may be *special*, limited to particular places or to particular forces, but of course can only bind the armies subject to the general who makes the truce, and co-extensive only with the extent of his command. This is all I ever claimed, and it clearly covers the whole case ; all of North Carolina was in my immediate command, with General Schofield, its department commander, and his army present with me. I never asked the truce to have effect beyond my own territorial command. General Halleck himself, in his Order, No. 1, defines his own limits clearly enough, viz.: " Such part of North Carolina as was not occupied by the command of Major-General Sherman." He could not pursue and cut off Johnston's retreat towards Salisbury and Charlotte without invading my command ; and so patent was his purpose to defy and violate my truce, that Mr. Stanton's publication of the fact, not even yet recalled, modified, or explained, was headed, " Sherman's truce disregarded," that the whole world drew but one inference. It admits of no other. I never claimed that that truce bound Generals Halleck or Canby within the sphere of their respective commands as defined by themselves.

It was a partial truce of very short duration, clearly within my limits and right, justified by events, and as in the case of prisoners in my custody, or the violation of a safeguard, given by me in my own territorial limits, I am bound to maintain good faith. I prefer not to change my report, but again repeat that in all future cases I am willing to be governed by the interpretation of General Grant, although I again invite his attention to the limits of my command, and those of General Halleck at the time, and the pointed phraseology of General Halleck's dispatch to Mr. Stanton, wherein he reports that he had ordered his generals to pay no heed to *my orders* within the clearly defined area of my command.

I am, yours,
W. T. SHERMAN, Maj.-Gen. U. S. A., commanding.

I now add the two letters written to Mr. Stanton at Savannah, and the dispatch from Atlanta mentioned in the body of my testimony, with Mr. Lincoln's answer:

HEADQUARTERS MILITARY DIVISION OF THE MISSISSIPPI,
In the Field, Savannah, January 2.

Hon. EDWARD M. STANTON, *Secretary of War, Washington, D. C.:*

SIR—I have just received from Lieutenant-General Grant a copy of that part of your telegram to him of 26th December, relating to cotton, a copy of which has been immediately furnished to General Eaton, my chief quartermaster, who will be strictly governed by it.

I had already been approached by all the consuls and half the people of Savannah on this cotton question, and my invariable answer has been that all the cotton in Savannah was prize of war, and belonged to the United States, and nobody should recover a bale of it with my consent; and that as cotton had been one of the chief causes of this war, it should help pay its expenses; that all cotton became tainted with treason from the hour the first act of hostility was committed against the United States, some time in December,

1860, and that no bill of sale subsequent to that date could convey title.

My orders were that an officer of the quartermaster's department, United States army, might furnish the holder, agent, or attorney a mere certificate of the fact of seizure, with description of the bales, marks, etc.; the cotton then to be turned over to the agent of the Treasury Department, to be shipped to New York for sale. But since the receipt of your dispatch I have ordered General Eaton to make the shipment himself to the quartermaster at New York, where you can dispose of it at pleasure. I do not think the Treasury Department ought to bother itself with the prizes or captures of war.

Mr. Barclay, former consul at New York—representing Mr. Molyneux, former consul, but absent since a long time—called on me in person with reference to cotton claims by English subjects. He seemed amazed when I told him I should pay no respect to consular certificates, and that in no event would I treat an English subject with more favor than one of our own deluded citizens; and that for my part I was unwilling to fight for cotton for the benefit of Englishmen openly engaged in smuggling arms and munitions of war to kill us; that, on the contrary, it would afford me great satisfaction to conduct my army to Nassau and wipe out that nest of pirates. I explained to him, however, that I was not a diplomatic agent of the General Government of the United States; but that my opinion so frankly expressed, was that of a soldier, which it would be well for him to heed. It appeared also that he owned a plantation on the line of investment to Savannah, which, of course, is destroyed, and for which he expected me to give him some certificate entitling him to indemnification, which I declined emphatically.

I have adopted in Savannah rules concerning property, severe but just, founded upon the laws of nations and the practice of civilized governments; and am clearly of opinion that we should claim all the belligerent rights over conquered countries, that the people may realize the truth that war is no child's play.

I embrace in this a copy of a letter dated December 31, 1864, in answer to one from Solomon Cohen, a rich lawyer, to General Blair, his personal-friend, as follows:

Major-General F. P. BLAIR, *Commanding Seventeenth Army Corps :*

GENERAL—Your note, inclosing Mr. Cohen's of this date, is received, and I answer frankly, through you, his inquiries.

First. No one can practise law as an attorney in the United States, without acknowledging the supremacy of our Government. If I am not in error, an attorney is as much an officer of the court as the clerk, and it would be a novel thing in a Government to have a court to administer law that denied the supremacy of the Government itself.

Second. No one will be allowed the privileges of a merchant; or rather, to trade is a privilege which no one should seek of the Government without in like manner acknowledging its supremacy.

Third. If Mr. Cohen remains in Savannah as a denizen, his property, real and personal, will not be disturbed, unless its temporary use be necessary for the military authorities of the city. The title to property will not be disturbed in any event, until adjudicated by the courts of the United States.

Fourth. If Mr. Cohen leaves Savannah under my Special Order No. 143, it is a public acknowledgment that he " adheres to the enemies of the United States," and all his property becomes forfeited to the United States. But as a matter of favor he will be allowed to carry with him clothing and furniture for the use of himself, family, and servants, and will be transported within the enemy's lines—but not by way of Port Royal.

These rules will apply to all parties, and from them no exception will be made.

> I have the honor to be, general,
> Your obedient servant,
>
> W. T. SHERMAN, Major-General.

This letter was in answer to specific inquiries. It is clear and specific, and covers all the points; and should I leave before my orders are executed, I will endeavor to impress upon my successor, General Foster, their wisdom and propriety.

I hope the course I have taken in these matters will meet your approbation, and that the President will not refund to parties claiming cotton or other property without the strongest evidence of loyalty and friendship on the part of the claimant, or unless some other positive end is to be gained.

I am, with great respect,

Your obedient servant,

W. T. SHERMAN,

Major-General commanding.

HEADQUARTERS, MILITARY DIVISION OF THE MISSISSIPPI,
In the Field, Savannah, January 19.

Hon. E. M. STANTON, *Secretary of War, Washington, D. C.:*

SIR—When you left Savannah a few days ago, you forgot the map which General Geary had prepared for you, showing the route by which his division entered the city of Savannah—being the first troops to occupy that city. I now send it to you. I avail myself of the opportunity also to inclose you copies of all my official orders touching trade and intercourse with the people of Georgia, as well as for the establishment of the negro settlements. Delegations of the people of Georgia continue to come, and I am satisfied a little judicious handling, and by a little respect being paid to their prejudices, we can create a schism in Jeff. Davis's dominions. All that I have conversed with realize the truth that slavery, as an institution, is defunct, and the only questions that remain are, what disposition shall be made of the negroes themselves. I confess myself unable to offer a complete solution for these questions, and prefer to leave it to the slower operations of time. We have given the initiative, and can afford to wait the working of the experiment.

As to trade matters, I also think it is to our interest to keep the people somewhat dependent on the articles of commerce to which they have been hitherto accustomed. General Grover is now here, and will, I think, be able to manage this matter judiciously, and may gradually relax and invite cotton to come in in large quantities.

But at first we should manifest no undue anxiety on that score, for the rebels would at once make use of it as a power against us. We should assume a tone of perfect contempt for cotton and every thing else, in comparison with the great object of the war—the restoration of the Union, with all its rights and powers. If the rebels burn cotton as a war measure, they simply play into our hands, by taking away the only product of value they now have to exchange in foreign ports for war-ships and munitions. By such a course, also, they alienate the feelings of the large class of small farmers, that look to their little parcels of cotton to exchange for food and clothing for their families. I hope the Government will not manifest too much anxiety to obtain cotton in large quantities, and especially that the President will not indorse the contracts for the purchase of large quantities of cotton. Several contracts, involving from six to ten thousand bales, indorsed by Mr. Lincoln, have been shown me, but were not in such a form as to amount to an order for me to facilitate their execution.

As to treasury trade-agents, and agents to take charge of confiscated and abandoned property, whose salaries depend on their fees, I can only say that, as a general rule, they are mischievous and disturbing elements to a military government, and it is almost impossible for us to study the law and regulations so as to understand fully their powers and duties. I rather think the quartermaster's department of the army could better fulfil all their duties, and accomplish all that is aimed at by the law. Yet, on this subject, I will leave Generals Foster and Grover to do the best they can.

I am, with great respect, your obedient servant,

W. T. SHERMAN,
Major-General commanding.

HEADQUARTERS MIL. DIV. OF THE MISSISSIPPI,
In the Field, Atlanta, Ga., Sept. 15, 1864.

Major-General HALLECK, *Washington, D. C.:*

My report is done, and will be forwarded as soon as I get a few more of the subordinate reports. I am now awaiting a courier from General Grant. All well, and troops in fine healthy camps, and supplies coming forward finely. Governor Brown has disbanded his militia, to gather the corn and sorghum of the State. I have reason to believe that he and Stephens want to visit me, and I have sent them a hearty invitation. I will exchange 2,000 prisoners with Hood, but no more.

W. T. SHERMAN,
Major-General commanding.

WASHINGTON, D. C., Sept. 17, 1864—10 A. M.

Major-General SHERMAN:

I feel great interest in the subjects of your dispatch mentioning corn and sorghum, and contemplated a visit to you.

A. LINCOLN, President U. S.

I have not possession here of all my official records, most of which are out West, and I have selected the above from my more recent letter-books, and I offer them to show how prompt and full have been my official reports, and how unnecessary was all the clamor made touching my action and opinions at the time the basis of agreement of April 18 was submitted to the President.

All of which is most respectfully submitted.

W. T. SHERMAN,
Major-General United States Army.

ANIMADVERSIONS UPON GENERAL SHERMAN,

WITH

A DEFENCE OF HIS PROCEEDINGS;

ALSO THE CALL FOR THE ASSEMBLING OF THE REBEL LEG-
ISLATURE OF VIRGINIA.

———

[*The following is the " Official War Gazette," forwarded to the newspapers by Secretary Stanton, and referred to in General Sherman's report, Part IV., and in his letter to General Grant, April 28, page 180.*]

WASHINGTON, April 22.

YESTERDAY evening a bearer of a dispatch arrived from General Sherman. An agreement for the suspension of hostilities, and a memorandum of what is called a basis for peace, had been entered into, on the 13th instant, by General Sherman with the rebel-General Johnston, the rebel General Breckinridge being present at the conference.

A Cabinet meeting was held at 8 o'clock in the evening, at which the action of General Sherman was disapproved by the secretary of war, by General Grant, and by every member of the Cabinet.

General Sherman was ordered to resume hostilities immediately, and he was directed that the instructions given by the late President in the following telegram, which was penned by Mr. Lincoln himself, at the Capitol, on the night of the 2d of March, were approved by President Andrew Johnson, and were reiterated to govern the action of military commanders.

On the night of the 2d of March, while President Lincoln and his Cabinet were at the Capitol, a telegram from General Grant was brought to the secretary of war, informing him that General Lee had requested an interview or conference to make arrangements for terms of peace. The letter of General Lee was published in the message of Davis to the rebel Congress.

General Grant's telegram was submitted to Mr. Lincoln, who, after pondering a few minutes, took up his pen and wrote with his own hand the following reply, which he submitted to the secretary of state and secretary of war. It was then dated, addressed, and signed by the secretary of war, and telegraphed to General Grant:

PRESIDENT LINCOLN'S INSTRUCTIONS.

WASHINGTON, March 3, 1865—12 P. M.

Lieutenant-General GRANT :

The President directs me to say to you that he wishes you to have no conference with General Lee, unless it be for the capitulation of General Lee's army, or on some minor and purely military matter.

He instructs me to say that you are not to decide, discuss, or confer upon any political questions. Such questions the President holds in his own hands, and will not submit them to military conference or conventions. In the mean time you are to press to the utmost your military advantages.

EDWIN M. STANTON, Secretary of War.

The orders of General Sherman to General Stoneman, to withdraw from Salisbury and join him, will probably open the way for Davis to escape to Mexico or to Europe with his plunder, which is reported to be very large, including not only the plunder of the Richmond banks, but previous accumulations.

A dispatch received from Richmond says : " It is stated here, by responsible parties, that the amount of specie taken south by Jeff. Davis and his party is very large, including not only the plunder of the Richmond banks, but previous accumulations."

They hope, it is said, to make terms with General Sherman or some other Southern commander, by which they will be permitted, with their effects, including their gold plunder, to go to Mexico or Europe. Johnston's negotiations look to this end.

After the Cabinet meeting last night, General Grant started for North Carolina to direct operations against Johnston's army.

EDWIN M. STANTON, Sec'y of War.

THE CORRESPONDENCE AND THE "MEMORANDUM"—REPORTED REASONS FOR THEIR DISMISSAL BY OUR GOVERNMENT.

WASHINGTON, April 23.

As reports have been in circulation, for some time, of a correspondence between Generals Johnston and Sherman, the following memorandum, or basis of what was agreed upon between the generals, and the result, is published :

MEMORANDUM or basis of agreement, made this, the 18th day of April, A. D., 1865, near Durham's Station, in the State of North Carolina, by and between General Joseph E. Johnston, commanding the Confederate army, and Major-General W. T. Sherman, commanding the army of the United States, both present.

First. The contending armies now in the field to maintain the *status quo* until notice is given by the commanding general of any one to his opponent, and reasonable time, say forty-eight hours, allowed.

Second. The Confederate armies now in existence to be disbanded and conducted to their several State capitals, there to deposit their arms and public property in the State arsenal; and each officer and man to execute and file an agreement to cease from acts of war, and to abide the action of both State and Federal authorities. The number of arms and munitions of war to be reported to the chief of ordnance at Washington city, subject to the future action of the Congress of the United States, and in the mean time to be used solely to maintain peace and order within the borders of the States respectively.

Third. The recognition, by the Executive of the United States, of the several State Governments, on their officers and Legislatures taking the oath prescribed by the Constitution of the United States; and when conflicting State Governments have resulted from the war, the legitimacy of all shall be submitted to the Supreme Court of the United States.

Fourth. The re-establishment of all Federal courts in the several States, with powers as defined by the Constitution and the laws of Congress.

Fifth. The people and inhabitants of all States to be guaranteed, so far as the Executive can, their political rights and franchise, as well as their rights of person and property, as defined by the Constitution of the United States and of the States respectively.

Sixth. The executive authority or Government of the United States not to disturb any of the people, by reason of the late war, so long as they live in peace and quiet, and abstain from acts of armed hostility, and obey the laws in existence at the place of their residence.

Seventh. In general terms, it is announced that the war is to cease; a general amnesty, so far as the Executive of the United States can command, on condition of the disbandment of the Confederate armies, the distribution of arms and the resumption of peaceful pursuits by officers and men hitherto composing said armies. Not being fully empowered by our respective principals to fulfil these terms, we individually and officially pledge ourselves to promptly obtain authority, and will endeavor to carry out the above programme.

W. T. SHERMAN, Major-General,
Commanding the Army of the United States
in North Carolina.

J. E. JOHNSTON, General,
Commanding Confederate States Army
in North Carolina.

It is reported that this proceeding of General Sherman was disapproved for the following among other reasons:

First. It was an exercise of authority not vested in Gen. Sherman, and, on its face, shows that both he and Johnston knew that General Sherman had no authority to enter into any such arrangements.

Second. It was a practical acknowledgment of the rebel Government.

Third. It undertook to re-establish rebel State governments that had been overthrown at the sacrifice of many thousand loyal lives and immense treasure, and placed arms and munitions of war in hands of rebels at their respective capitals, which might be used as soon as the armies of the United States were disbanded, and used to conquer and subdue loyal States.

Fourth. By the restoration of rebel authority in their respective States, they would be enabled to re-establish slavery.

Fifth. It might furnish a ground of responsibility on the part of the Federal Government to pay the rebel debt, and certainly subjects loyal citizens of rebel States to debts contracted by rebels in the name of the State.

Sixth. It puts in dispute the existence of loyal State governments, and the new State of West Virginia, which had been recognized by every department of the United States Government.

Seventh. It practically abolished confiscation laws, and relieved rebels of every degree, who had slaughtered our people, from all pains and penalties for their crimes.

Eighth. It gave terms that had been deliberately, repeatedly, and solemnly rejected by President Lincoln, and better terms than the rebels had ever asked in their most prosperous condition.

Ninth. It formed no basis of true and lasting peace, but relieved rebels from the presence of our victories, and left them in a condition to renew their efforts to overthrow the United States Government and subdue the loyal States whenever their strength was recruited and any opportunity should offer.

[Appended is the Editorial from the New York " Times," April 24th, alluded to in General Sherman's letter to General Grant, April 28th—p. 181.]

GENERAL SHERMAN'S EXTRAORDINARY NEGOTIATION FOR PEACE.

THE loyal public will read with profound surprise the terms which General Sherman tendered to the rebel Government, as represented by its only uncaptured commander, General Johnston, as the basis of peace. In reading the provisions of this remarkable compact—which was signed on the 18th of April, four days after the assassination of President Lincoln—one is at a loss to know which side agreed to surrender. Johnston certainly could have intended nothing of the kind. He evidently believed himself to be negotiating with an equal—dictating terms, rather than receiving them—and laying the basis of a new Government, based on a theory of State rights as absolute and complete as Calhoun ever dreamed of.

No plea need be sought to justify the rebellion and all the atrocious acts that have followed in its train, beyond that which is found in this scheme of pacification. The title of the "Confederates" to an equal *status* with the national authorities is conceded in the first article of the agreement; and that infamous concession is stanchly supported in the second article, which, instead of providing for the surrender of the rebel arms and munitions of war to the United States Government, expressly provides for their deposit in the State arsenals under the keeping, and subject to the orders, of any new league of conspirators that may arise hereafter.

In his wildest flights of imagination, in his boldest schemes of burglary, Floyd himself never conceived a plan or basis for a new rebellion superior to this. A difficulty between the United States Government and some foreign power would be the signal to every unarmed rebel to hie to the State arsenal and equip himself for a new attempt to throw off the authority of the Government, and realize the dream of a slave Confederacy.

The fifth article in the agreement is intended not only to secure full amnesty for every class of rebel offenders, but to open the way for the re-establishment of slavery in all the seceded States. It is a provision running in the face of the most important legislative enactments and executive decrees that have come into force since the rebellion commenced. It changes, at one stroke, the whole policy of the national Government. It substitutes for the formal resolutions of Congress, and the solemn decisions of the national Executive, the compromises of a military subordinate with a rebel leader. It carries the nation back to the very source and fountain of the calamities which were sprung upon it when the guage of battle was first thrown down by the conspirators. It undoes all that has been found politic in asserting the supreme authority of the government; all that has been esteemed righteous and humane in the discomfiture of slavery; all that has been considered essential to justify the honor and uphold the justice of the national cause before the world. And to each separate clause of this ignoble instrument, which, by

the connivance of a weak and recreant Executive, might
have become the *Magna Charta* of American slavery,
General Sherman gave the sanction of his name, as the immediate representative of the military power of the United
States.

The act, viewed in its purely military bearing, must be
regarded as one of most dangerous insubordination. Had
there been no express orders to direct Gen. Sherman, the
terms of surrender accorded by Lieutenant-General Grant
to Lee were available as a guide to the subordinate general.
The prime feature of that surrender was illustrated in the
brief and emphatic report of Grant to the War Department:
" *There has been no relaxation in the pursuit during its
pendency.*" How did the subordinate in this case follow
the example of his superior? By a prompt concession of
an armistice to his crafty opponent—a concession which, as
it was the first eager thought of Lee, was naturally like-
wise the prime consideration with Johnston and his illus-
trious mentors, Davis and Breckinridge. On that concession depended all the hopes of personal safety of these
fugitives from justice. On that concession depended their
ability to show the "sympathizing" outside community
that, before they resigned their posts as Confederate leaders,
the *status* of the Confederacy was formally acknowledged
by a United States commander, next to the highest in rank
in the national army.

But General Sherman had more than the example of his
immediate chief to guide him, if he desired to escape the
grave charge of insubordination. He had before him the
direct injunctions of the late President, which directly for-
bade the discussion of political terms of settlement between
military commanders and rebel leaders. So long ago as
the 3d of March—the very closing day of President Lin-

coln's first term—Secretary Stanton was instructed to write to General Grant that the President desired him "to have no conference with General Lee, unless it be for the capitulation of Lee's army, or on some minor and purely military matter." If a transcript of this absolute injunction was not made, textually, for Sherman's guidance, the injunction itself was perfectly known to him, and he was well aware that powers of negotiation were not denied to the lieutenant-general to be conceded to one of his subordinates.

We fear that this most unfortunate step of General Sherman has already led to results of serious detriment to the national cause. It has probably allowed Davis and Breckinridge, with their prominent and responsible confederates in the rebellion, to secure their personal safety; and there is some reason also to apprehend that it may have allowed Johnston to remove his army beyond the immediate reach of his late antagonist. Its worst effects, however, were averted by the prompt and peremptory intervention of the President; and we hope that the presence of the lieutenant-general, who set out for North Carolina before midnight on Friday, may obviate all the serious evils which it was calculated to involve.

[*The dispatches of General Halleck and Secretary Stanton, on the violation of General Sherman's truce, referred to in the Report, Part IV., and the Examination, are as follows.*]

WAR DEPARTMENT,
Washington, D. C., April 27—9.30 A. M.

Major-General DIX :

The department has received the following dispatch from Major-General Halleck, commanding the Military Division of the James :

Generals Canby and Thomas were instructed some days ago that Sherman's arrangement with Johnston was disapproved by the President, and they were ordered to disregard it, and to push the enemy in every direction.

EDWIN M. STANTON, Secretary of War.

RICHMOND, Va., April 26—9.30 P. M.

Hon. EDWIN M. STANTON, *Secretary of War* :

Generals Meade, Sheridan, and Wright are acting under orders to pay no regard to any truce or orders of General Sherman respecting hostilities, on the ground that Sherman's agreement could bind his own command and no other.

They are directed to push forward, regardless of orders from any one except General Grant, and cut off Johnston's retreat.

Beauregard has telegraphed to Danville that a new arrangement has been made with Sherman, and that the advance of the Sixth Corps was to be suspended until further orders.

I have telegraphed back to obey no orders of Sherman, but to push forward as rapidly as possible.

The bankers here have information to-day that Jeff. Davis's specie is moving South from Hillsboro', in wagons, as fast as possible.

I suggest that orders be telegraphed, through General Thomas, that Wilson obey no orders from Sherman ; and notifying him and Canby, and all commanders on the Mississippi, to take measures to intercept the rebel chiefs and their plunder.

The specie taken with them is estimated here at from six to thirteen millions.

II. W. Halleck, Major-General commanding.

[*The subjoined article, written in defence of General Sherman against the above attacks, appeared in the Washington " Chronicle," May 25th, and is attributed to the pen of his brother, Senator Sherman.*]

[For the Daily Chronicle.]

SHERMAN AND STANTON.

A quarrel between two high officers of the Government is always unfortunate, unseemly, and usually injurious to each. This is especially so when they are working in the same great cause, and that cause brilliantly successful— crowned with a glorious peace. It is idle to conceal evidences of passion eagerly promulgated by the telegram and press, and it is well for kindly lookers-on to take a dispassionate view, to see if all this heat is necessary. The writer of this knows both parties, and is certainly friendly to each.

The commencement of any difference was with the Sherman-Johnston convention. This, if approved by the President, would have made peace between the Potomac and Rio Grande. The objections made to this are included in three propositions : 1st, That Sherman had no power to make such a treaty. The answer is obvious, that he never

9*

claimed or attempted to conclude the arrangement. All he did "conclude" was a truce for a few days; and he then submitted, for the approval or rejection of the President, this important offer of a general peace. Even in arranging the truce he had it all on his side. Wilson was still moving and holding the outer coils of the net, while Sherman was building railroads and repairing roads and bridges, ready for the final spring if the arrangement was disapproved. He gained every thing by the truce, and lost nothing. Johnston was "corelled," and was kept so by this very truce, while Sherman was never more active in preparing for future movements, if necessary. It is said generals have no business to make truces or deal with political questions, and that Grant was reproved for this; but Sherman had made truces before, and for a year has been distinguished for his treatment of political questions, without a word of caution or reproof from his superiors. The telegram to Grant, now published as an official order of an old date, was withheld from Sherman, and Sherman had been instructed to open communications with rebel civil authorities.

The second objection is that the arrangement recognized the rebel State government and officials. This is the most serious objection, and amply justified the Government in rejecting or modifying the arrangement; but the official papers show clearly that Sherman refused to grant this in any shape or form, until the order of Weitzel, issued while Mr. Lincoln was present in Richmond, convened the rebel Legislature of Virginia and recognized the rebel Governor Smith. With this order before him, without a word of the contrary tenor, Sherman informed Johnston of the order, and waived his previous objection to recognizing the rebel State authorities. Why should Sherman be denounced for submitting to the new President a proposition based upon this order, of the revocation of which he had not the least notice ? How unjust to arraign him for this, and then conceal the fact that he was acting in pursuance of the policy of the former Administration !

The third objection is that he recognized slavery, and restored the old relations between master and.slave. This is simply absurd. Sherman has repeatedly acted upon the validity of the proclamation of emancipation and the laws of Congress abolishing slavery, and the idea of repealing or strengthening them by a military arrangement between the generals never entered his head. The official papers show that he urged Johnston to announce as a "fact" the extinction of slavery—a "fact" that Sherman not only regarded as fixed, but as unalterable. The result was, that slavery was not mentioned, but was left precisely where it ought to be left. The nervous fear that this question could not be left to the law and the Supreme Court did not disturb a purely military mind.

This was the arrangement about which so much has been said. It disbanded the rebel armies, placed all their arms within our power, made peace universal ; and it was purely conditional, having no life without the approval of the President. Now it is plain that the duty of the Government was to simply approve or reject it, and give no reasons, but issue its orders, *and this is precisely what was done by the President, and he did no more.* General Grant was sent to convey this order, and did his duty nobly and well, with generous consideration for his subordinate and fellow-soldier. Sherman did not hesitate a moment, promptly terminated the truce, made a new arrangement with Johnston, and at once started for Charleston and Savannah, to send supplies to General Wilson, then far in Georgia, and to close up the scattered links of his great command. His official report shows an amount of zeal, activity, patriotism, and wonderful ability not surpassed by any portion of his previous life. All this was going on while he was in utter ignorance of the wild storm of denunciation that was sweeping over the whole country. While he was supplying Wilson, arranging to catch Davis, detaching armies from his command, and preparing for peace and home, the press and the telegraph, the pulpit and the rostrum, were ringing with denunciations. A letter of a rebel to the London · *Times* was universally quoted as the revelation of a plot to overthrow the Government. Cromwell and Arnold, and all that was desperate and violent, was suddenly brought to public notice. To defend Sherman, and even to beg people to " wait—let us hear from him," was to invite quarrel and insult. Timid people were pitying him and all connected with him. People who had slept soundly in their beds at night and made money every day during the war, thought General Sherman had joined the " Copperheads," and was no better than Jeff. Davis, and even hinted that he had got some of Jeff. Davis's gold.

General Sherman first met this " chilling wind" as he was coming northward around Cape Henry, to meet his army and surrender his command.. He was then writing his official report. He firmly believed that all this fierce and most unreasonable calumny was organized by Mr. Stanton and General Halleck, with the deliberate purpose to insult, humiliate, and ruin him. He then first saw Stanton's reasons and Halleck's insulting order. He mixed all the falsehoods and malignity with these two official acts. No wonder that this gave tone to his official report, and under this shadow it should be read. It will soon be made public, and the writer of this ventures to predict that every fair-minded man who contributed to the clamor will, on reading it, regret his part.

The rejection of the convention and the reasons of Stanton were given to the public at the same moment. They had the appearance of contemporaneous acts; but they were entirely distinct and separate. The fact of disapproval was sent by Grant, and was entirely legitimate, and resulted well. Grant even did not know these "reasons." Not a shade of discontent could have arisen. Why, then, publish these reasons? The answer of Mr. Stanton is, that General Sherman's order announcing the truce tô his army made it necessary—that he could not disappoint the hopes of the army, based upon this order, without giving the reasons; that he got a·copy of the order after Grant left, and then penned these reasons. The gloom of the public mind, and his own escape from assassination, no doubt colored his statement, and suspicion aroused by a desperate crime, lit upon the most conspicuous person who, at the moment, seemed to thwart the national cry for vengeance. Sherman's arrangement breathed the spirit of the dead President; but it came one week too late, or one month too early. In either contingency Stanton's reasons would never have been issued. They were his alone, and are plainly marked with passion, but may have been published without malice.

But, it is said, why did Sherman issue this order to his troops? Why did he assume that peace was to exist from the Potomac to the Rio Grande? Why not wait until the arrangement was approved? The answer is, that it was necessary to announce the truce to the army to prevent collision and loss of life. The order was to the army only, and expressly stated that the truce depended upon the approval of the President. Without a knowledge of the truce how could officers or men perform their new duties, and in what better terms could a conditional truce be expressed? Sherman talked to his army alone, merely for their temporary action. Can any man read the order now without approving it?

Then followed the advice of Halleck to ignore Grant, to insult Sherman, and to arrest the movement of subordinate officers, not only without the knowledge but in defiance of both of them. And this was accompanied by the military offence of Halleck's disregarding a truce, and actually invading another military department to assault an enemy under terms of surrender. It was fortunate that this order was countermanded in time, or an actual collision might have occurred, in violation of a truce, between two armies of our noble heroes. For this General Halleck ought alone to be held responsible. If he was of any service at all other than an expensive luxury, tried and labelled away where it was supposed he was harmless, he should, as a writer on military law, have been the last man to advise the breach of a truce—the soldier's "higher law." He knew that Johnston had surrendered, was awaiting the action of the President upon that surrender, and that Grant, his superior officer, was conveying that action to Sherman; and yet he advised a course that could only be justified by the clearly ascertained fact that both Grant and Sherman were traitors to their country.

And then, why publish this order? What motive could possibly induce this? If some grave exigency justified the order, it should have been kept secret as the grave. If they found Sherman was playing the traitor, their precautions should have been concealed. In any aspect, the publication of this paper seems the grossest folly or the meanest malice. If justified by events, it was a blunder to publish their plans; but when viewed by the light of events, it was a most gross public insult heaped upon a soldier while in the successful discharge of the highest duties. The writer of this does not know that either Stanton or Halleck authorized its publication, but he does know the withering effect it had upon Sherman's reputation, not for what was alleged in it, *but from what was fairly implied from it.* Why is not this explained? Who published it? Where was the public censor then? Why not now announce in an equally specific order that the fears upon which it was based proved utterly groundless? If Mr. Stanton published this order, and will not now openly acknowledge that it was founded in error, he continues an insult and evinces malice. Then he must expect open defiance and insult, and neither his person nor rank can shield him.

It cannot be denied that after this order was issued, while the telegraph was under a strict military censorship, the public mind was poisoned against General Sherman by telegrams since shown to be false, as that he refused to obey the summons of the Congressional committee; and that facts relieving him from blame were not stated, as that the order of General Weitzel was approved by Mr. Lincoln, but afterwards withdrawn. And this, too, while General Sherman was beyond the reach of letter or telegram, actively engaged in his official duties. It is true that Mr. Stanton neither can or ought to control the press, and is often roughly handled by it. Yet had not an officer in General Sherman's position the right to expect some effort on the part of his department to stay the tide of calumny, the very moment the return of General Grant with the unconditional surrender of Johnston proved how groundless and foolish had been the idle fears at Washington?

Now, it is plain that the true course is to publish the official report; to respect the natural resentment of a soldier sensitive on account of a palpable wrong ; to avoid mingling personal feelings with the general joy over great triumphs; to neither force nor oppose public judgment upon the merits of a controversy no longer important to the nation, and leave to the country and history to settle the credit due to the prominent actors in the war. The writer of this is not disposed to belittle either the services of General Sherman or the energy of Mr. Stanton, and would rather see both expended on the common enemy.

THE CALL FOR THE ASSEMBLING OF THE REBEL LEGISLATURE OF VIRGINIA.

[As General Sherman was influenced to introduce into the "memorandum" of agreement entered into with General Johnston the recognition of State governments, from the permission given by the Federal authorities for the meeting of the Virginia Legislature, the "call" for such meeting is here given. This is prefaced by the order of President Lincoln to General Weitzel, authorizing such permission. The order was handed to General Weitzel by Senator Wilkinson on the morning of April 7th. General Weitzel afterwards saw the committee who prepared the "call," which he approved for publication. On the 12th, the day after its promulgation, General Weitzel received a telegram from President Lincoln, in Washington, to annul the call, as the necessity for it had passed.]

HEADQUARTERS ARMIES OF THE UNITED STATES,
City Point, April 6, 1865.

Major-General WEITZEL, *Richmond, Va.:*

It has been intimated to me that the gentlemen who have acted as the Legislature of Virginia, in support of the rebellion, may now desire to assemble at Richmond and take measures to withdraw the Virginia troops and other support from resistance to the General Government. If they attempt it, give them permission and protection, until, if at all, they attempt some action hostile to the United States; in which case you will notify them, giving them reasonable time to leave, and at the end of which time arrest any who remain. Allow Judge Campbell to see this, but do not make it public.

Yours, etc.,
A. LINCOLN.

TO THE PEOPLE OF VIRGINIA.

The undersigned, members of the Legislature of the State of Virginia, in connection with a number of the citizens of the State, whose names are attached to this paper, in view of the evacuation of the city of Richmond by the Confederate Government, and its occupation by the military authorities of the United States, the surrender of the Army of Northern Virginia, and suspension of the jurisdiction of the civil power of the State, are of the opinion that an immediate meeting of the General Assembly of the State is asked for by the exigencies of the situation.

The consent of the military authorities of the United States to a session of the Legislature in Richmond, in connection with the governor and lieutenant-governor; to their free deliberation upon public affairs, and to the ingress and departure of all its members under safe conduct, has been obtained.

The United States authorities will afford transportation from any point under their control to any of the persons before mentioned.

The matters to be submitted to the Legislature are, the restoration of peace to Virginia, and an adjustment of the questions involving life, liberty, and property, that have arisen in the State as a consequence of war.

We therefore earnestly request the governor, lieutenant-governor, and members of the Legislature to repair to this city by the 25th of April instant.

We understand that full protection to persons and property will be afforded in the State; and we recommend to peaceful citizens to remain at their homes and pursue their usual avocations with confidence that they will not be interrupted.

We earnestly solicit the attendance in Richmond, on or before the 25th of April instant, of the following persons, citizens of Virginia, to confer with us as to the best means of restoring peace to the State of Virginia.

We have procured safe conduct from the military authorities of the United States for them to enter the city and depart without molestation.

The Hons. R. M. Hunter, A. T. Carpenter, Wm. C. Rives, John Letcher, A. H. H. Stuart, R. L. Montague, Fayette M. Mullen, J. P. Holcombe, Alexander Rives, B. Johnson Barbour, James Barbour, Wm. L. Goggin, J. B. Baldwin, Thomas S. Gholson, Walter Staples, Thomas J. Randolph, Wm. T. Early, R. A. Claybrook, John Critcher Williams, T. H. Eppes, and those other persons for whom passports have been procured, and especially others whom we consider it unnecessary to mention.

A. J. MARSHALL, senator from Fauquier.
JOHN WESSON, senator from Marion.
JAMES VENABLE, senator elect from Petersburg.
DAVID J. BURR, of the House of Delegates, from Richmond.
DAVID J. SAUNDERS, of the House of Delegates, Richmond city.
D. S. WALL, of the House of Delegates, Wetzel county.
J. J. ENGLISH, of the House of Delegates, Henrico county.
Mr. AMBERS, of the House of Delegates, Chesterfield county.
A. M. KEITZ, House of Delegates, Petersburg.
H. W. THOMAS, second auditor, Virginia.
Lieutenant L. L. MONCURE, chief clerk, second auditor's office.
JOSEPH MAYO, mayor, city of Richmond.
ROBERT S. HOWARD, clerk Hustings Court, Richmond city.
THOS. W. DUDLEY, sergeant, Richmond city.
LITTLETON TAZEWELL, Commonwealth's attorney, Richmond city.
WM. T. JAYNES, judge of the Circuit Court of Petersburg.
JOHN A. MEREDITH, judge Circuit Court, Richmond.

WM. H. LYONS, judge Hustings Court, Richmond.

WM. C. WICKHAM, member of Congress, Richmond.

BERRY S. EWELL, president William and Mary Collège.

NAT. TYLER, editor Richmond *Enquirer*.

R. F. WALKER, publisher *Examiner*.

J. R. ANDERSON, Richmond.

R. R. HOMISON, Richmond.

W. GODDIN, Richmond.

P. G. BAGLEY, Richmond.

F. J. SMITH, Richmond.

FRANKLIN STEMS, Henrico.

JOHN LYON, Petersburg.

THOMAS B. HEISHER, Fauquier.

WM. M. HARRISON, Charles City.

CYRUS HALL, Ritchie.

THOS. W. GARNETT, King and Queen.

JAMES A. SCOTT, Richmond.

I concur in the preceding recommendation.

J. A. CAMPBELL.

Approved for publication in the *Whig*, and in handbill form.

G. WEITZEL,
Major-General commanding, Richmond, Va.

April 11, 1865.

LETTER FROM GENERAL SHERMAN.

[The following characteristic letter, addressed to Colonel Bowman, of Washington, forms an appropriate conclusion to this work.]

. CAMP NEAR ALEXANDRIA, VA., May 19.

DEAR BOWMAN—I am just arrived. All my army will be in to-day. I have been lost to the world in the woods for some time. Yet, on arriving at the "settlements," found I had made quite a stir among the people at home, and that the most sinister motives have been ascribed to me.

I have made frequent official reports of my official action in all public matters, and all of them have been carefully suppressed, while the most ridiculous nonsense has been industriously spread abroad through all the newspapers. Well! you know what importance I attach to such matters, and that I have been too long fighting with real rebels, with muskets in their hands, to be scared by mere non-combatants, no matter how high their civil rank or station.

It is amusing to observe how brave and firm some men become when all danger is past. I have noticed on fields of battle brave men never insult the captured or mutilate the dead; but cowards and laggards always do. I cannot now recall the act, but Shakespeare records how poor Falstaff, the prince of cowards and wits, rising from a figured . death, stabbed again the dead Percy, and carried the carcass aloft in triumph to prove his valor. So now, when the rebellion in our land is dead, many Falstaff's appear to brandish the evidence of their valor, and seek to win applause, and to appropriate honors for deeds that never were done.

As to myself, I ask no popularity, no reward; but I dare the War Department to publish my official letters and reports. I assert that my official reports have been purposely suppressed, while all the power of the press has been malignantly turned against me.

I do want peace and security, and the return to law and justice from Maine to the Rio Grande; and if it does not exist now, substantially, it is for state reasons beyond my comprehension. It may be thought strange that one who has no fame but as a soldier, should have been so careful to try to restore the civil power of the Government, and the peaceful jurisdiction of the Federal courts; but it is difficult to discover in that fact any just cause of offence to an enlightened and free-people. But when men choose to slander and injure others, they can easily invent the facts for the purpose when the proposed victim is far away, engaged in public service of their own bidding. But there is consolation in knowing that, though truth lies at the bottom of a well, the Yankees have perseverance enough to get to that bottom.

Yours truly,

W. T. SHERMAN.

www.ingramcontent.com/pod-product-compliance
Lightning Source LLC
Chambersburg PA
CBHW020611030726
47497CB00007B/2191